T0082739

MURAROOT

E. Thornton Goode, Jr.

MURAROOT

iUniverse books may be ordered through booksellers or by contacting:

iUniverse
1663 Liberty Drive
Bloomington, IN 47403
www.iuniverse.com
844-349-9409

ISBN: 978-1-6632-2229-9 (sc)
ISBN: 978-1-6632-2230-5 (e)

Library of Congress Control Number: 2021908782

Print information available on the last page.

iUniverse rev. date: 04/29/2021

In Appreciation

The story is being told by the character, James. I want to thank my friend, Paul Tanner, for the use of his picture, so the reader can have a likeness of the character, James.

My friend, Galen Berry, has allowed me to use his picture, so the reader may see what the character of Ricardo looks like. Galen is an incredible artist and pianist. His marble art is amazing.

Another friend who is allowing me to use his picture is Alejandro Barbosa. He will give you the likeness of the character, Miguel, the operator of the helicopter.

And last but not least, I want to thank my friend, Steve Young, for letting me use his pictures, so the reader may get an idea as to the likeness of the character, Muraroot.

Thank you, Steve.

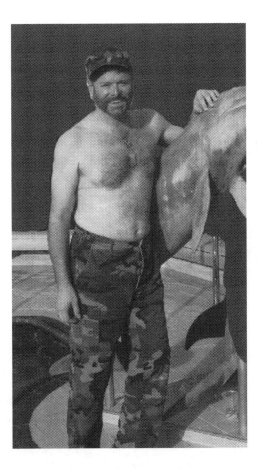

Biographical Information

I love living on the SW coast of Mexico. It is wonderful here. Retiring here was one of the best decisions I have made in my entire life. Moved down here in 2014 after retiring and selling the house in the Atlanta, Georgia area in 2013.

This is novel number four to go to press. First was <u>The</u> <u>Old</u> <u>Lighthouse</u> in December 2007, then <u>The</u> <u>2</u> in January 2012 and lastly <u>Two</u> <u>Portraits</u> <u>in</u> <u>Oil</u> in February 2020. After this one, there are eight more in line.

Prologue

Do you know what a Ouija Board is? I'm sure you do. But just in case you don't, here's a picture of one.

A planchette is used on the board to point out letters, numbers and information. The older planchettes were made of wood. The newer ones are made of plastic. Sometimes in movies, you'll see an inverted wine glass used as one.

Ouija boards, gypsy fortune tellers and psychic readers play a role in this story. Many are extremely skeptical of them. I definitely understand. But I must tell you. Because of certain happenings in my own life, I've become a believer. Two books have also influenced my thinking on the subject. One is <u>Lessons from the Light</u> by George Anderson and the other is <u>Many Lives, Many Masters</u> by

Brian Weiss. Trust me. They're both very interesting books and well worth reading.

Yes. Believe it or not, I've gone to a psychic reader. I was quite skeptical at the time and kept looking for flaws in what she told me. But this lady said things there was no way she could have known. There's no way she could have researched me. She had no clue I was even coming to have a reading till I was there. Not to mention, she was from England and had arrived in Atlanta only about a week before. Yeah.

It's like the old Shakespearean line from Hamlet. "There are more things in heaven and earth, Horatio, than are dreamt of in your philosophy." So true. So true.

This novel is about a party, being held by James, the best friend of a central character, David. It is the summer of nineteen eighty-nine. James has invited many of his good friends over to tell them the story of David's great adventure and how the supernatural and a psychic came into play, making predictions and giving information, leading many of the central characters to their Destiny.

Listen. The party has begun and you, too, have been invited. Have a seat and get comfortable. Unfortunately, you won't be able to ask any questions. Just listen carefully. Should you have any, those questions will most likely be answered in time. James shall begin very shortly right after some necessary information for you to think about as the story progresses.

CHAPTER I

"Hey! Farley! Want something to drink? I'm going to run get a soda." Bob got up from his seat.

"No. I'm fine. Thanks for asking." Farley looked at Bob and smiled.

After a while, Bob returned with his drink and sat in a seat across from his friend. He quickly looked around at the other people, sitting at the gate, waiting to board the plane. "Well, Farley. What have you thought of the trip so far? I think it's been totally cool."

Farley nodded. "Yeah, man. I'm so glad the school arranged for it to happen. You know trips like this don't happen every day. I'll bet it took some doing to arrange games with all these schools down here. But what an adventure."

"Yeah. I'm sure glad we have an interpreter with us. I understand coach speaks some. I'd sure hate for us to come across as the ugly Americans." Bob gave a big grin.

"I know what you mean. Not only are we getting the chance to play soccer with teams that really know the game but we're getting a chance to know those our own age in foreign countries. That's so hip."

Bob took a drink of his cola. "I think it's so groovy. Let's see. Our next game is the day after tomorrow. That'll give us a chance to rest up for a day after we get there later this evening." He paused for a moment. "Plane was supposed to leave at eight this morning. How much more time is it before we board?"

"Should be leaving here in less than thirty minutes. I see the rest of the guys seem to be anxious. They keep looking up at the clock on the wall. Yeah. A nine-hour flight. With the change in time zones and all, we should get us in around seven tonight."

Bob turned around and looked at several of those in the group. "I'm surprised there aren't more people. Looks like only eight other people so far besides all of us. We'll virtually have the whole plane to ourselves. I think that's so cool."

Farley responded. "That's all right with me. Maybe I'll be able to catch up on a little shut-eye during the flight since we had to get up so early this morning to catch this flight."

It wasn't long until there was an announcement for boarding. Everyone grabbed their carry-on luggage and headed out the door.

Bob commented. "Farley. How do you like this weather down here? It's the bomb."

"Yeah. It's great. Warm but great."

Shortly, all were at the plane and climbing the steps to the door. Everyone entered and in no time at all were seated.

Bob noticed where his friend was sitting. "Farley! On all the flights we've taken, you seem to choose a seat in the same area of the plane every time. What is that?"

"It's the seats near the wings. I've always heard it's the strongest part of the airplane."

A questioning look came to Bob's face. "The strongest part of the airplane?"

"Yeah. In case something should happen."

Bob shook his head. "Okay. Cool. If you say so."

At that moment, the engines started up. Slowly, the plane began to move forward.

Bob looked out the window. "Wonder how many RPMs those propellers turn?"

"I don't know. Just as long as it's fast enough to keep us in the air." Farley began to laugh.

Everyone on the plane heard both comments and began to laugh.

The plane had been aloft for just over two hours when Bob turned to his right and looked out the window. He was sitting in the seat right behind his friend. "Farley. Check out your window. Looks like one wingding dilly of a storm, coming up from the south. And look at all that lightning."

Just then, an announcement came over the intercom system. It was from the captain. Everyone in the group looked at one another with questioning expressions. None understood a word.

The group's interpreter understood. He got up and stood in the aisle. "The captain was just explaining. They're going to divert to the north to try and avoid the upcoming storm. He also said he was sorry that it will delay our arrival somewhat. He wants everyone to fasten your seat belt." He returned to his seat.

Bob called out. "Now, more than ever, I'm glad we have a whole day to rest before the game."

Even with the plane's change of course, the storm quickly caught up with it. It was incredibly fierce. The plane was being tossed around like a rag doll. With every major jerk, everyone let out a short cry of anxiety.

Suddenly, a team member, sitting across from Bob, was thrown out of his seat, landing in the aisle.

Bob yelled out. "Farley! I think Rick's hurt!"

"No problem! I'll get him back in his seat." Getting up, Farley grabbed Rick off the floor and put him back in his seat, snugly tightening his seat belt. "He's a little out of it but I think he's going to be okay." He turned to return to his seat.

Just then, the plane tossed violently, throwing Farley up against the ceiling and then down onto the floor. His head hit very hard and he went almost unconscious.

"Farley!" Bob cried out. He and another teammate quickly got up, pulled Farley off the floor and strapped him tightly in the seat on the aisle. They quickly returned to their own seats as fast as they could and strapped in.

In a few seconds, Farley spoke. "Geez. What happened? Wow. That was a bummer."

Bob responded. "Glad you're okay. You got a nice bump on the head."

For virtually an hour, the plane continued to lurch and jerk, being severely tossed around. All conversations had stopped.

Suddenly, Bob began to hear the loud sounds of twisting metal and the popping of rivets. He knew this was not a good thing. "Farley! Man! That don't sound good at all!"

Bob was absolutely correct. He looked around as the plane began to disintegrate before his eyes. Everyone began to scream.

Bob cried out. "FARLEY!"

CHAPTER II

James stood up. "Everyone! Please, get a plate and fix yourself a croissant sandwich. All the fixings are on the table over there." He pointed to the dining area of the large living room dining room combination. "Albert will get you a cocktail. When you've done that, please, be seated and we'll begin."

All present quickly went to the table and got what they wanted. Soon, all returned to their previous seats.

"I see everyone is ready. Excellent. If you want more sandwiches, please, get up and get some. That's no problem. You'll still be able to hear what I'm saying and that's important, so you know the whole story. Also, later, there will be a break for about ten minutes or so. You can hit the 'john' if you need to."

This brought a nod from everyone with sounds of approval.

James walked over to the fireplace, turned and tapped his cocktail glass several times with the ring on his left hand. The sound filled the room, catching everyone's attention. He gave a big smile. "You, my friends, have been invited here tonight for a specific reason. I want to tell you a story. But first, I must ask you this. How many of you believe in Fate and Destiny? How many of you believe in such things as psychic readers? Fortune tellers? Ouija boards?"

James began to snicker. "Sorry. I can't help it. But believe it or not, these things are part of the story I'm about to tell you. It concerns two friends of mine as well as my Albert and myself." He glanced in Albert's direction and smiled. "Some of you know them but many of you don't. And of whom am I speaking? They're two friends who are very close and dear to me. One I've known since we were kids."

"I brought you here to tell their story and for you to meet them. As I get into it, many of you will realize you've heard some of this before, possibly in news reports four years ago. Also, in a special done by my friend, Donald." He gestured in the direction of one of the guests. "He'll tell you more, later on."

"Now. Let me see. It was back seven years ago in nineteen eighty-two. David won the lottery in November of that year. It virtually set him up for life." He looked around at everyone in the room. "I see several of you who know him are nodding and smiling."

A voice came from the group. "Ah, James. If I remember correctly, weren't you somehow in on that as well?"

James acknowledged the guest. "Michael. It seems YOU do remember." He shook his head. "But I'll get more into that later. Let me continue."

"Mason." He smiled, bent his head down, shaking it. "Now, there's one for the books. His story is so far out in left field, you'd think it would air as a TV special movie. What can I say?"

"Well. They arrived yesterday and are staying at their house in town. I told them they were invited to a party tonight to meet all of you and to arrive around nine. I asked you all here at five, so it would give me some time to tell you all their story and give you something to eat in the meantime." James paused for a moment. "Yes. David still maintains the house here in town, so they have a place to stay when they come in. Most of the time, they stay at their main house, using it as a jumping-off place. If you don't know what I'm talking about, I'll explain as I go on."

"I think back, remembering it all and it seems so strange. As I said, who'd have ever believed a Ouija board, a gypsy fortune teller and a psychic reader would have a hand in it? But, they did. As a matter of fact, I was there the night we played with the Ouija board for the first time."

James took a sip of his cocktail. He looked at his glass. "During the time I'm telling the story if you need a refill of your cocktail, just raise your hand and Albert will gladly get you another. Albert doesn't really have to hear the story. He and I have been together forever and he knows both of them. He knows their whole story as well."

Albert brought another cocktail for James and set it on the table next to him.

James smiled at Albert. "Thank you, Albert." He looked out at everyone. "All should be so fortunate to have a man like Albert as his partner." He bowed his head toward Albert.

All smiled, clapped their hands and cheered.

After a few moments, James looked around the room and saw everyone was ready. He smiled and tilted his head slightly upwards. The expression on his face was one of searching for some lost memory. "As I mentioned, David and I have been friends forever, growing up in Virginia. Around Richmond. So you understand it all, I guess I should really start back then. Yes. We were thirteen. It was the summer of nineteen fifty-eight. Rock 'n' Roll had already begun. Yes. I'm sure everyone remembers thirteen. That's when boys started getting interested in girls."

There was a slight snicker in the room, slowly growing into loud laughter, clapping of hands and slapping of knees.

"Okay. Okay. SOME were interested in girls." James nodded to the three lesbian couples in the room as everyone looked their way, clapping and cheering. "BUT! Most of us… WE were all interested in boys. What can I say?"

The room erupted with loud cheers, clapping, hoots and whistling.

When it calmed down, James smiled. "I shall continue." He paused for a moment. "It was a stormy night and I was having a sleepover at David's. He'd used his allowance to buy a Ouija board and we decided to use it for the first time."

David walked over to the dresser in his bedroom, opened the bottom drawer, pulling out and holding up a Ouija board and planchette. "James. Look what I bought last weekend. There was a booth out in the parking lot at the grocery store, being run by gypsy folks. The gypsy lady told me to use it very carefully."

A questioning expression came to James' face. "Don't tell me you believe in that shit?"

"You're nothing but a filth mouth. Don't let my mom hear you say stuff like that. You know she'll tell your mom."

"Fucking 'A'. Yeah." James started laughing out loud. "I do have to admit a Ouija board is pretty cool."

"The gypsy lady said I should never use it alone. Not sure why. After I bought it, I happened to turn it over. Look." David turned the back of the board in James' direction.

James clapped his hands together. "Hot shit! Looks like someone's initials."

"James! I swear." David shook his head. "Now. She said if two people are using it, both people should sit in a chair, facing one another with the board on their knees. They can also place it on a small table between them. If more than two, they should put the board on a small table and all sit around it, so everyone can put their fingers on the planchette. Want to try it?"

"Fuck yeah, man!" James gave a big grin and flexed his eyebrows.

"You do know one of these days you're going to slip and say one of those words in the wrong place and your mom's going to tell your dad and he's going to beat the shit out of you."

"Ah… Did I just hear you say 'shit'?" James gave a big grin.

"Okay. Okay. So, you got me. Now, get that chair over there and let's try this thing."

They both got comfortable with the board on their knees. David placed the planchette in the center of the board.

James spoke quietly. "This is like the beginning of one of those spooky horror movies."

They both giggled.

"Okay. Let's get this show on the road." James insisted.

"She also said something about asking for a guide. Not quite sure what she meant, either. But I know we both have to put our first two fingers of both hands on the planchette when we ask questions." David looked down at the board.

They both put their fingers on the planchette and were silent for a moment.

James spoke quietly and looked right at David. "Maybe we should see if someone's out there. I think you should ask the questions since it's your board."

"Okay. Good idea." David looked up and around the room then spoke quietly. "Is anyone out there?"

Still keeping their fingers on the planchette, they waited for a few moments. Suddenly, the planchette moved slowly to 'YES', paused for a moment then moved back to the center of the board.

David looked at James. "You pushed it!"

"No! I swear, man! I didn't!"

"Really?" David looked around the room. "Maybe there really is someone out there."

"Ask who it is." James was insistent.

"Okay." David paused for a moment. "Who are you? Do you have a name?"

The planchette moved to 'YES' and after a few seconds, started moving across the board. In unison, James and David called out each letter. "'I'. 'S'. 'H'. 'M'. 'A'. 'E'. 'L'. Ishmael?" The planchette went to 'YES' then moved back to the center of the board again.

A questioning look came to James' face. "Isn't that the character in Moby Dick? You know? The guy who tells the whole story?"

David looked scornfully at James. "That Ishmael was a fictitious character, not a real person."

James looked at David, around the room then down at the board. "Excuse me. Do you see a real person in the room other than us?"

David couldn't help but shake his head.

James was ecstatic. "Ishmael. Wow. That's so totally groovy."

David spoke. "Hello, Ishmael. Welcome to our Ouija board. I'm David and this is my friend, James."

The planchette began to move. 'HELLO DAVID HELLO JAMES'. It stopped for a moment then began to move again. As it did, they watched the next word being formed. Then, the planchette stopped, moving to the center.

"It spelled 'AGE'." David shook his head. "Do you want to know our ages?"

The planchette moved to 'YES'.

"James and I are both thirteen."

The planchette moved again, spelling out more words. 'I AM LAUGHING I REMEMBER 13'.

James and David were curious. "How old are you?"

'VERY OLD'.

James jumped in. "What's it like where you are?"

'JUST WAIT YOU WILL SEE ONE DAY'.

David asked another question. "Do you have any words of wisdom for us?"

'YES REMEMBER 11'. There was a pause before the planchette moved again. '12'. Again, there was another slight pause. Then, it moved again. '1982'. Then, there was a series of numbers with short pauses in between. '12'. '23'. '56'. '73'. '82'. After an extended pause, there was another number. '3'.

James tilted his head. "'Eleven'. That must be November. 'Twelve'. That's the day. And the year is 'Nineteen Eighty-Two'. What do you think? Not sure what the other six numbers are but I'm sure they'll have some meaning someday. Especially, since they're related to November, nineteen eighty-two." He paused for a moment then yelled. "Holy Shit! Fuck! We'll be damned old! Thirty-seven! Old as dirt!"

"Damn, James! Watch your mouth! One day. Yeah. One day it's going to get you in deep trouble."

James raised his eyebrows. "Hey! You said 'DAMN'." A huge grin filled his face.

"I swear." David shook his head. "Okay. Okay. I think you're right."

With their fingers still on the planchette, David asked another question. "Ishmael. You want us to remember November twelfth, nineteen eighty-two and these six numbers?"

The planchette moved to 'YES'.

James was insistent. "David, you keep a journal. Write all that down."

David ran over and opened the bottom drawer of his dresser, got out his journal, opened it then put his fingers back on the planchette. "Ishmael, could you repeat the numbers again slowly, so I can write them down? Thank you."

As the numbers were slowly repeated on the Ouija board, David wrote the date and numbers down.

He set his journal aside and put his fingers back on the planchette. "Geez. Thanks, Ishmael. We surely appreciate that. Anything else for us?"

The planchette moved to 'NO NOT RIGHT NOW'.

"Ishmael. I have one more question. The two letters on the back of the board. Are they someone's initials?"

The planchette moved. 'YES BUT NOT TO WORRY THAT WILL BE REVEALED IN TIME IT IS NOT IMPORTANT RIGHT NOW'.

"Okay. Thanks. We'll let you go for now but we'll check back with you again, soon. Take care of yourself. Later."

The planchette moved to the bottom of the board and pointed to 'GOOD BYE'.

David took the board and the planchette, putting them in the bottom drawer to his dresser. "Wow. That was so cool."

James shook his head. "You know no one will believe us."

David agreed. "Who cares? We know it happened and that's all that matters. Now, I think it's time for us to hit the hay before mom comes up here and wonders what we're doing."

"Yep. I think you're right. Anyway, it's getting late. What do you want to do tomorrow?"

"We could run down to the grocery store and see if the gypsies are still out in the parking lot." David suggested.

"Yeah. And you can tell the lady there we contacted a person named Ishmael."

As they lay in bed, James spoke softly. "Nineteen eighty-two. Damn! That's a fucking long way off."

David quietly called out from his bed. "James!"

James just snickered. "Well. It is." He continued to snicker.

After a while, all was quiet and they were finally asleep.

James took a drink of his cocktail, smiled and shook his head. "If you're curious, we did go to the grocery store the next day. There was no sign of the gypsy folks in the parking lot."

He took another sip of his cocktail. "Yep. We had no idea how important that date and those numbers were at that time."

Michael raised his hand and called out. "Weren't those the numbers, winning you and David a bundle back in nineteen eighty-two?"

"Michael. You're very astute. But let's not get ahead of ourselves in the story."

Michael continued. "Ah. Wait. And what about the initials? Do you ever find out what they are and who they belonged to?"

James just smiled. "Michael. Patience. Patience. You'll understand soon enough."

Everyone chuckled.

After a few moments, James began again. "Well, over the next few years, David and I got out the Ouija board and Ishmael came back each time. But there was no new information. Ishmael just continued to tell us about the same date and numbers and not to forget them."

"In the summer of nineteen sixty-two, again, we got out the Ouija board. Ishmael brought up the date and numbers as he usually did but this time he mentioned a name. 'LORIE'. He indicated that a woman named Lorie would soon come into our lives and would give us more information at that time."

CHAPTER III

James continued. "It was May of nineteen sixty-three. David and I were Seniors in high school. We'd be graduating in less than a month. The host for the Seniors' Party had an unexpected guest. He thought it would be fun for everyone. The guest was a psychic reader. All those who might be curious could go to her and have a reading done. Her name? Lorie."

"When we heard her name, we almost fell over. Both of us were extremely interested in meeting her and hearing what she might have to say."

James looked at David. "I'll go first. Then, you can go. How's that?"

"Cool. Come get me when you're done." David headed to the munchies table.

James walked over to Lorie. "Hey, Lorie. I'm James. Okay. I'm game." He smiled.

Lorie smiled. "Great, James. They have a room set up for me down the hall. Come on. Let's go check it out. You're the first one who's wanted to have a reading."

James looked over at David, standing at the munchies table, flexed his eyebrows as he gave a big grin and a 'thumbs-up' with his right hand. He followed Lorie down the hall to a secluded room.

There was a card table in the middle of the room with a chair on either side. They both sat down.

Lorie looked right at James and smiled. "Have you ever done this before?"

James gave a huge grin. "Ah. You're the psychic. You should know that." He chuckled

Lorie smiled. "Interesting. We have a skeptic here."

"Well. Not a skeptic. I've just heard about those who do this and are total scammers. But to answer your question. No. But I've always thought it would be so cool. Now, David and I have played with a Ouija board before. Does that count?"

Lorie nodded. "Well. Similar but not quite the same."

After a moment, she spoke again. "First, I want you just to relax and feel comfortable. Then, I want you to clear your mind. I'm going to do the same. During this session, if you have any questions, please, feel free to ask them." After a few moments, she smiled. "Okay. Are we ready?"

James gave a big grin and a 'thumbs-up'. "You bet! Let's do it!"

She started off, telling information about his previous years. Then, she went into some past life experiences which James really enjoyed hearing. He loved the part where he was a Roman soldier.

"Yes. You're a Roman soldier. During that time period, you have a very close friend who's another Roman soldier." Lorie smiled. "It seems you both have been together in many past lives as good friends. He's with you even now. He's your good friend even today."

James responded. "You must be talking about David. When we first met as kids, there was an immediate connection between us."

"Yes. It's all those past lives shared together as friends. You'll be friends for life and... even into future lives." She paused for a moment. "There's coming a time he'll rely greatly on your friendship and expertise. Yes. I'm not sure what that means. But I see dollar signs." She paused. "Maybe you're going to make him some money somehow."

"I see you're going to college. Yes. Virginia Tech. Engineering."

A questioning look came to her face. She shook her head. "No. No, Business. Yes. I see. You're intended to be a financier and stockbroker." She grinned. "Maybe I was right about you making David some money." She paused briefly. "I still see engineering connected to you for some reason. Humm." She shook her head. "Graduating with honors, you'll be hired by a very good financial and brokerage firm in a large city in the south. I'm pretty sure it's Atlanta. Now, it makes sense. Being a financier, you'd be involved with investments and stocks. Yes. That could be where you make David some money."

"In the early seventies, you're going to meet someone very special. Oh. Now, I see why I connected engineering with you at first. This person is going to be an engineer and from what I can see, you both will be together for life. I see the letter 'A' associated with him."

"Interesting." A strange look came to her face. "All of a sudden, a date has come to me. November twelve. Wait. It's November twelfth, nineteen eighty-two. I get nothing more, regarding that date and have no idea what it means. I'm so sorry about that but it must be important to you for some reason. Remember it." After another questioning pause, she continued. "Does the name Ishmael mean anything to you?"

James was shocked. There was the date from the Ouija board and hearing Ishmael's name. "Ishmael? You have to be kidding." He shook his head. "Ishmael has been our guide when we use the Ouija board. Tell me if that's not weird as shit?" He grimaced for a second. "Sorry about that."

Lorie smiled and chuckled. "Not a problem. Maybe he came to me to let you know he's not a fake."

James snickered. "Maybe he came to let me know YOU'RE not a fake, too."

They both laughed.

Lorie paused. "By the way, it seems you're going to do very well as a financier and stockbroker. Very well indeed." After another pause, she gave a big smile. "James. That's all I see for you right now that's significant. I hope it helps. Do you have any questions?"

"No. But my friend, David, wants to have you do his reading. I can go get him and send him in." He stood up. "Thank you very much. This was very interesting. Very interesting. I appreciate the information you gave me and I will remember it."

Lorie smiled. "I'm glad you enjoyed it. And if you'd get your friend, that would be fine."

James turned, left the room and walked down the hall. He walked over to David. "I'm pretty sure this bitch is for real. I don't think she's a fake. She said some real interesting shit. She even asked me about Ishmael. Yeah. Now, it's your turn. She's waiting."

David could see on James' face the session had had a profound effect on him. "Okay. When I'm done, we'll have to compare notes." He turned and headed down the hall to the room where Lorie was waiting.

He walked in, smiled and stretched out his right hand. "I'm David. Nice to meet you."

Lorie stood and they shook hands. "Yes. Please, sit down, relax and we'll begin." She gestured to the chair across the table from her. "I have to admit. Your friend's a real crackerjack." She shook her head.

David just shook his head and smiled. "What can I say?"

They both laughed.

"Well. Now, I'm not going to break any confidences I shared with him. If he desires to do that, it'll be his decision. You two have known each other for a very long time. I tell you now, you both will be friends for life and beyond."

"I see from several past lives, you and James have been friends many times. There's always been a great trust and companionship with him."

"In virtually all your past lives, you've always sought truth and have always wanted people to do the same. You despise lying and dishonesty." She paused for a moment and looked directly at David.

"By the way, if you should have any questions, during the session, please, don't hesitate to ask."

She tilted her head and a questioning look came to her face. "There's a man. No. Not James. This man has been in several past lives with you. He's very significant. You've always been more than just friends or companions. I believe you haven't met him yet in this life. But you will."

After a pause, she changed the subject. "I see you're going to attend Virginia Tech. You'll be studying architecture and art. You'll even go into the Master's program in art. This is due to your teachers encouraging it. They see you do excellent work. When you leave school, you'll be moving to a large southern city. Interesting. It'll be a city where James is already living. Atlanta. I'm pretty sure."

A shocked look comes to her face. "I don't believe it. A date has come to me. I saw the same date in connection with James. November twelfth, nineteen eighty-two. Again, I have no knowledge as to what it means but it's obviously of significance. Yes. I know I said I wouldn't share any confidences I shared with James but this is just too unbelievable to be coincidence."

David interrupted. "Before I came in here, James said you mentioned the name, Ishmael. Every time we used the Ouija board, Ishmael was our guide. He has mentioned that date numerous times. James and I aren't sure of its significance, either."

Lorie looked right at David. "Well, I'd definitely circle that date on your calendar and when it comes, be aware of every minute."

"I now see the ocean. Beautiful beach with black rocks, sticking up out of the sand and water. It appears to be volcanic rock. Do you go to a beach like this?"

"No. But I love the beach. The ones I've been to are like Nags Head, Virginia Beach and Daytona. None of those have black rocks."

"Interesting. Whatever it is, it's important and will be significant to you."

Suddenly, Lorie was jolted in her chair with shock. "Oh, my

God! Wow!" She paused and was breathing hard. "This is uncanny. Creepy. I don't believe it."

David was in suspense. "What? What is it?"

"I'm so sorry but this is truly bizarre. You're not going to believe it. I don't believe it. But I just got the same snake image I got several years ago, doing a reading. And just like his, it's not a live snake. It's a carving. Yes. It looks like stone."

David was surprised. "So, that's really unusual?"

"You bet. Especially, when it involves those who don't know one another. With friends like you and James, possibly. But not like this. Wow! Yes. And it's near water. Also, just like before, there's a group of people associated with this. Yes. They're dark-skinned with black hair and dressed in native type clothes. They have the appearance of the Indians of the Old West." She shook her head. "I don't believe it. It's exactly like what I saw in the other reading."

Lorie continued. "Oh! Wow! Now, this is totally new and wasn't part of the other reading. There's a warrior. Tall. No. Not a warrior. A hunter. Yes. Holy cow! Yes. Tall, brown hair and facial hair. Very well-built. I see him, carrying a spear and dressed like the other people. But his skin isn't dark like the other people." Then, she cried out. "Oh, my God! It's the man! The one I saw in your past lives! HE is the hunter! No wonder you haven't met him yet. He doesn't even know who he is. I have no clue why."

"I see the letter 'M' associated with him. No! Wait! Now, it's the letter 'F'. Wait. This is very strange. I see the two letters, bouncing back and forth. This is very confusing. I'm not sure exactly what it means. Sorry, I can't be more helpful with this."

David was taken totally by surprise. He remembered. Those were the two letters on the back of the Ouija board. How weird was that? But he didn't interrupt.

"There's something very strange about this man. He just doesn't seem to belong where he is. Yes. I see. When you meet him, you're going to be a major factor in figuring out this puzzle. He's a little older than you in this life. Wait! I see green. A jade green color. I'm not sure what that means as I only see the color."

Lorie sat quietly for a few moments. "Wow. That was extremely weird. What can I say?"

David questioned. "When did this happen? The other reading. Do you remember?"

"Let me see." Lorie tilted her head and looked up, trying to remember. "It was. It was like three years ago. June of nineteen sixty. Up in New England. Yes. I'd been invited to a graduation party quite similar to this one. It was a young man at the party. But I don't remember anything else about him or his reading. Sorry."

She was silent for a few seconds. "Well, David. Nothing else is coming to me right now. It seems I've given you everything you need to know for the moment. In time, I believe many of the things I've mentioned to you, you'll finally understand. I must admit. I believe the significance of both of you having the same image in your readings is a sign to let you know he's the one you seek in this life."

David looked at Lorie and smiled. "The information you've given me has been very informative. Thank you so very much for taking your time with me. I gratefully appreciate it."

David got up and opened the door to the room. "There's no one waiting, so you might just as well come on out and join the party. I'm sure if someone else wants to have a reading, they'll come over and ask you."

They both left the room and walked down the hall to the party.

James had been patiently waiting for David to come out. He was very interested in what Lorie had to tell him. Finally, he saw David and Lorie come from the hallway. He ran over and grabbed David's arm, pulling him aside. "Okay. I want to hear. 'Enquiring minds want to know.'"

They both grabbed a soft drink and went out onto the front porch. David revealed all Lorie had told him.

"Wow. Tall, furry face, well-built and in some skimpy loincloth. YeeeHaw! Sounds all right to me. Sounds like someone who's right up your alley." James slapped his knee. "Now. That's very interesting about the two letters, 'M' and 'F'. Maybe his name is Mother Fff..."

"JAMES! I swear. You have to make everything into something vulgar." David paused for a moment. "But... THAT is funny."

They both broke into loud laughter.

"Wait a minute." James continued. "If I remember correctly, those are the two letters on the back of your Ouija board. And she had no explanation?"

"Nope. She had no clue."

"Interesting. Very interesting. Okay. What about the date?" James persisted. "She didn't tell me anything more about the date. Hey. We've still got nineteen years to figure it out. Have to tell you, the snake thing is really strange. Especially, when she's had it before. Yeah."

David responded. "Yes. She even got freaked out about it. And the date. She made it quite clear the date was very significant for both of us. But she never mentioned or said anything about the numbers. I guess we may figure that out in time."

James took the last sip of his cocktail and set it on the nearby table just as Albert delivered a fresh one. James smiled at him. "Thank you, Albert."

Just then, Michael raised his hand and spoke. "James. When you were younger, you must have been one filth mouth."

Everyone roared with laughter.

"Michael. Thank you for bringing that to our attention." James shook his head.

Michael stood up and took several bows.

Everyone continued to laugh, cheer and clap.

When the room calmed down, James continued. "Yes, we both graduated in early June of sixty-three. That whole summer was a gearing up for heading off to Tech. We talked about being roommates but decided to let the Fates take a hand in who we'd share a room with. After all, we'd be meeting guys from all over. It would be an expanding of our thinking."

"It was late August when we headed off to college. It was for Freshman orientation before the fall quarter began. By Thanksgiving, we'd both settled into our curricula. My business classes were going well just as were David's architecture and art classes."

"In time, Lorie's words came to pass. By spring quarter, we both were doing exceedingly well in our fields. My professors were seeing my potential and directing me to take certain advanced classes. It was the same for David. His professors were extremely astonished at his artistic abilities. His artworks were amazing. They, too, were directing him to more advanced classes."

"It's funny. I remember when we were Juniors, David's profs wanted him to submit some of his works in an art show. What was so special is the show was held every spring but usually just for the Seniors. Yep. The works would also be for sale if the artists wanted it so."

James knocked on the door of David's dorm room. "David. It's me."

David opened the door. The telltale smell of turpentine was detectable.

James sniffed. "I'm surprised your roommate hasn't tossed your ass out with that fucking turpentine smell permeating everything."

"He doesn't mind it. He tells me great artists need to be given leeway for their creativity."

"Well, I'm glad he's SO understanding." James looked around the room. "Damn. You have eight canvases done and you're working on another one?"

"Yeah. I'm giving Jackson Pollock a run for his money with this one. Just to prove I, too, can drip and throw paint at a canvas."

At that, he picked up his brush and flicked some phthalo green at the canvas, sitting on the easel. He then put the brush in the jar of turpentine.

They both just snickered.

James smiled. "Wanted to see if you were hungry. Heading to the cafeteria for some dinner."

David wiped his hands on the cloth, hanging on the easel to remove the bit of oil paint on them. "Yeah. I need a break, anyway. Josh should be coming in from class soon."

Just as David uttered the words, Josh opened the door and walked in. "Hey, James. How are you?"

"Doing fine. Came to see if David wanted to go eat. Why don't you come with us?"

"Sounds good." He put his books on his desk and looked around the room. "I swear. David's so amazing. Look at those incredible landscapes and still life paintings he's done. He should get a pretty penny for them at the show. Mark my words. He's going to be famous one of these days." He looked at the canvas on the easel. "If I didn't know any better, I'd swear Jackson Pollock sneaked in here and did that canvas."

They all started laughing and headed to the cafeteria.

James shook his head and took a sip of his cocktail. "Are you ready for this? David didn't put prices on any of his works for the show. He placed a box in front of each painting for potential buyers to slip in a piece of paper, containing their phone number, name and how much they wanted to pay for the painting. After the show, whoever submitted the highest price for each work would be sold the painting."

James giggled. "You're not going to believe it but the Jackson Pollock style painting sold for the highest price of all."

Laughter filled the room.

"I will mention his other ones didn't sell cheap, either. David made enough money on all of them to cover the cost of his three previous years of school. Yeah. And those, who submitted bids during the show, were very interested in commissioning him to do some paintings for them at some point in time down the road. He did just as well in the spring of his Senior year." James paused. "And just so you know. Since Josh had been so understanding about David's work, David did a large landscape for him and gave it to him. Josh was ecstatic. He said he'd have it for the rest of his life on his living room wall wherever he lived."

"We both graduated in June of sixty-seven and I headed out to my first job. Again, Lorie was correct. An established financial group hired me as a financier and stockbroker. And yes, it was here in Atlanta."

"As for David at the urging and suggestions of virtually all his professors, he stayed for two more years in the graduate program. They were so amazed at his style and technique with oils. Many said they'd never seen such superb artistry in a student."

"After completing his studies, a prestigious architectural firm wanted him to come work for them. Yep. You guessed it. It was here in Atlanta. I told David to stay with me while he got settled. That would give him time to look for a place of his own."

"He continued doing canvases as several galleries around the country were requesting to show and sell his works. He usually has several in Roger's gallery in Midtown. Go by and check it out." He nodded and gestured toward one of the guests and smiled.

"Yes. Life was good for the both of us. I was doing very well and making my clients quite happy with their investments. Even David wanted me to invest his savings. We were both doing very well."

"Then, there came that night in the summer of nineteen seventy-three. We were twenty-eight."

CHAPTER IV

David hung up the phone and turned to James. "James. Why don't we go out and celebrate? That was the gallery in New York, calling to let me know they sold a wonderful still life. YeeeHaw! Roger called me yesterday and wants me to bring him a few more as well. I sure could use a nice cocktail. Dinner, too."

"What can I say? Sounds good to me!" James clapped his hands.

They headed to a place they knew well and enjoyed. The Armory. The age group there varied but most of the customers were business, professional and working people. Another thing they liked. There was a great restaurant associated and connected with it called The Prince George. At the restaurant, they knew the host, the bartender, the piano player and most of the waiters. They also found the food quite excellent.

It was a usual Saturday night at The Armory. The place was quite lively with customers. Seeing James and David come in, the bartender virtually had their drinks ready by the time they reached the bar.

"Thanks, Johnny." James placed a twenty-dollar bill on the bar then raised his hand to Johnny and smiled as he grabbed both drinks, handing one to David.

"James. Thank you. You are always way too kind." Johnny smiled back and nodded.

James smiled and turned to David. "I swear. Gay men make the best bartenders. They see you come in, know your drink and have it ready by the time you reach the bar. I wonder if that happens in straight bars?" He grinned. "Doubt if I'll ever find out."

David was very fond of James and his generosity. He was always kind and thoughtful. David remembered him saying many times 'good service demands good rewards'. James always gave a gratuity of twenty to twenty-five percent to a waiter or server if he did a good job. Sometimes even more.

They took their drinks and headed across the room to the wall shelf called the 'meat rack'. It was called that because it was a place one could stand, put down your drink and see and peruse the entire room. It made it easy for others in the room to see you as well and was a comfortable place to be when all the seats at the main bar were taken.

While standing there, James began to slowly scan the room and those sitting at the main bar. That's when he saw a man, sitting and leaning against the bar. He was facing the floor area. James' mouth fell open in awe.

David saw this happen and started to chuckle. "Okay. Who do you see? Your tongue is hanging out so far, it's almost on the floor. Put it back in your mouth before you step on it."

James spoke softly. "It's that guy over there. At the bar. He's so fucking handsome. Geez."

David looked in the direction James was peering. He had to admit. The guy was very attractive. "Why don't you go over and introduce yourself?"

James turned to David with a terrified expression on his face. "I can't do that."

A questioning look came to David's face and he tilted his head to the side. "Why not? YOU of all people. Mr. Confidence and Self-Assured."

"I just can't." He shook his head.

"Sure you can." David grabbed James' arm and started dragging him toward the handsome man, leaning back against the bar. Finally, they were in front of him. David looked down at the man's smiling face. "I hope you don't mind but my friend here would very much like to meet you and say hello."

The man looked up at James with a huge smile. "Well, hello. I'm Albert." He stuck out his right hand.

James smiled. "James." He extended his hand, shaking Albert's. "And this is my friend, David." David and Albert shook hands. James continued. "I've not seen you in here before."

Albert smiled. "Well, believe it or not, I've been here a few times and I've seen you. I understand you're in finance and stocks."

James was quite taken aback and shocked. "Why, yes. That's correct. But... I..." He shook his head. "I swear. I'd have definitely remembered you if I'd seen you. How could I not have seen you? Damn."

Albert smiled, slapped his right knee then spoke with conviction. "It wasn't time yet. We weren't supposed to meet... until now."

Surprise and awe came over James' face. "Wow. Geez. You believe in that stuff, too? Wow! I hope we can become friends." James paused then with surprise, he cried out. "Albert! Your name begins with an 'A'! Could you be the one Lorie was talking about?" He was totally surprised. "You don't happen to be an engineer, are you?"

Albert smiled. "Well. I have no clue who Lorie is but I have a feeling we'll become a lot more than just friends." He flexed his eyebrows several times. "Yep. I'm an engineer."

A giant smile filled James' face and his eyes opened wide.

David was extremely surprised at Albert's comment. "Ah. Excuse me. But why would you say that? I mean. That it wasn't time."

Albert shook his head. "Okay. I'll tell you but you must promise not to laugh."

David and James looked at one another and then back at Albert again.

"It's Destiny. Believe it or not, when I was in college, a traveling carnival came through the town. Those things have always fascinated me, so I went. While walking around, I came across a tent set up with a gypsy fortune teller. There was a sign in front of the tent. 'Know your future! Madame Zelda knows all!' I snickered to myself and said 'what the heck'." Albert giggled. "Actually, I said 'what the fuck'."

They all laughed and Albert continued. "Oh. Why not go in and see what my future was going to be."

James interrupted. "Pardon me for the interruption but have you eaten dinner yet?"

Albert looked up. "Why, no. Not yet."

"David and I were going next door to eat and I'd like to know if you might like to come with us? Something tells me we have much to talk about and I'd prefer doing it with food and cocktails. And not to worry. Dinner's on me."

David instantly interrupted and looked at James. "Ah. Excuse me. Dinner is on ME. Remember. It was MY painting that sold and I invited YOU to dinner. And since you seem to be meeting… your Destiny, YOU'RE not paying." He turned to Albert. "Albert. Please. Will you join us for dinner? And it's on me. When Destiny knocks, you need to open the door and you shouldn't have to pay." He gave a big smile.

Albert grinned. "Such a deal. Such a deal. Sounds great to me. Thank you very much for the invitation."

David smiled. "We always go right next door to eat. Everything there is superb. The food, drinks, service and piano playing are wonderful and excellent."

As they headed out, James waved at Johnny. "Johnny. Thanks again. Have a good evening."

Johnny smiled and waved. "James, thank you. Y'all take care now. Ya hear?"

It was just a short walk to the restaurant next door.

Opening the door, the host, George, was there to meet them. "Gentlemen. How have you been? James. David. Good to see you all again." He looked at them and smiled. He turned to Albert. "And who do we have here?"

James smiled. "This is Albert. And I have a feeling you may be seeing a lot more of him and me." His smile grew to a huge grin.

George turned to Albert. "Albert. Welcome to The Prince George. I hope you enjoy being here." He stepped back "Table for three? Excellent. Would you like to check with Jake and get a cocktail first?"

James smiled. "George, that would be terrific."

They walked to the bar.

"Hey, guys." Jake handed James and David their cocktail. He looked at Albert. "And what can I get for you, handsome Sir? And by the way. My name is Jake."

Albert shook Jake's hand. "I'm Albert. A gin and tonic would be great."

"One gin and tonic, coming up." Jake smiled.

Albert grinned. "It's totally obvious you both frequent this place often." He looked at the two cocktails Jake had presented to them. "You know. Gay men make the best bartenders. I swear."

David looked at James, then at Albert and all broke out in laughter.

David shook his head in the affirmative. "James made the same comment earlier this evening. And I wasn't kidding. The food and service here are excellent."

Jake handed Albert his drink. "Hope it's to your liking." He gave a big grin.

"Thank you, Jake." He took a sip, raised his glass in the air and smiled. "Excellent."

Jake gave a huge grin. "Thank you, my good man."

David immediately placed a twenty and a five on Jake's bar, nodded and smiled. "Jake. Thank you."

Jake smiled. "David. Thank you."

While walking to the table, David called to the piano player. "Patrick. How are you this evening? Good to see you again." He gave Patrick a big smile and dropped a twenty-dollar bill in his glass, sitting on the edge of the piano.

"David. Thank you. You're always so kind." Patrick continued to play and smiled. "Good to see you and James again. Hope all is well with you."

George continued to lead them to a table and placed a menu in front of them as they sat down. "Darrell will be with you shortly." He turned to leave the table.

As George left, David and James spoke in unison. "Thank you, George."

George turned, slightly bowed and smiled as he walked away.

David grinned. "I already know what I want."

James looked over at Albert. "I know what it is. He orders it virtually every time we come in here."

Albert looked down at his menu. "I've not eaten here before. Never took the time. But I've heard it was very nice." He looked over the selections. "Wow. The Delmonico sounds great."

James giggled. "Bingo! That's what I usually get. And trust me, it'll be prepared perfectly to your satisfaction. I guarantee it."

Darrell came up to the table and smiled. "Gentlemen. So good to see you all again. I hope you've been well. And what can I get you tonight?" Finally getting their order, he left the table.

James took a sip of his drink. "Okay. So. To continue. You went to a gypsy fortune teller. Wow. That's very interesting. Keep going."

Albert continued. "Yep. I've always believed in stuff like that. Yeah. I know there are fakes out there. You just have to be careful. But it's the ones who tell you stuff you know, yet there's no way in hell they could know anything about it. When that happens, you've found the real deal."

James broke into the conversation. "David and I went to see a reader back when we were Seniors in high school. She said some very interesting things that have actually come to pass." James took another drink. "But it really started back when we were thirteen. Yeah. David bought a Ouija board and we started using it."

David agreed. "James is correct. We were thirteen at the time. I bought it at a booth out in the parking lot of a grocery store. It was run by gypsies."

Albert smiled. "I've had several encounters with a Ouija board. A friend and I used to use one back when I was in high school. We had a guide. Yeah. His name was Ishmael."

James was taking a sip of his drink at that moment and almost choked when he heard the name. He started coughing.

David cried out with a boisterous outburst. "WHAT!?" He reached over and patted James on the back several times. Suddenly, realizing he'd been quite loud, he looked around the restaurant at the other patrons. He nodded and smiled with apology, mouthing 'sorry'. He was absolutely shocked at what he heard.

Darrell even came over to see if everything was all right. David reassured him all was well and was sorry for the outburst.

James finally got himself together and shook his head. "Ishmael? You have to be shitting me?"

Albert was totally confused. "What's wrong? I don't understand."

James shook his head. "I wonder if it's the same one who was our guide?" He looked questioningly at David.

Albert was astonished. "Really? Your guide was named Ishmael, too? You have to be kidding? No way!"

David nodded. "Well. How many Ishmaels could possibly be out there? Wow." He was very surprised. "Maybe we three need to pull out the board again and see."

Albert shook his head in the affirmative. "You still have the Ouija board? Wow! Not a bad idea. That could be fun."

"If you don't have plans for tomorrow, why don't you come over tonight and we can try?" James suggested.

Albert smiled. "I'd love to."

David directed the conversation back to the subject. "Tell us more about the gypsy fortune teller woman."

Albert took a drink of his cocktail. "My roommate and I were Freshmen in college. That's when we went to see her. At a traveling carnival. She told me I'd graduate and get a very good engineering job after moving to Atlanta." He paused, taking a sip of his cocktail. "She also said I'd meet someone who'd be very special." He paused again with a big grin on his face. "And his name would start with a 'J.'"

They all looked at one another in surprise.

"Yeah. She said he'd be in finance." Albert looked at James and flexed his eyebrows several times with a big grin on his face.

James' mouth fell open in shock. "You're kidding? You ARE kidding? The reader that David and I went to said I'd meet someone special. An engineer. And we'd be together for life. And she saw an 'A' associated with him."

Albert gave another big grin and flexed his eyebrows several times again. "Interesting. Very interesting."

They all just quietly laughed.

David raised his glass. "Here's to Ouija boards, psychic readers and gypsy fortune tellers."

Everyone raised their glasses and clinked them together. All called out. "Hear! Hear!"

James raised his glass in the air. "Yep. If David hadn't dragged my ass over to the bar, it might never have happened. So, now you know. That's how I met my Albert, the love of my life." He toasted in Albert's direction.

Everyone raised their glasses and cheered. "Hear! Hear!" "Hear! Hear!"

"I must tell you. We all went home that night and got out the Ouija board. Strangely enough, we were going to discover something interesting about Ishmael."

David called out as he headed to his bedroom. "James, fix us all a cocktail while I go get the Ouija board."

James and Albert headed to the kitchen to get some glasses. After filling them with ice, they headed to the bar.

David came out and cleared everything off the end of the coffee table. He then took three pillows off the sofa, placed one on either side of the coffee table and the last one at the end. That way, all would be able to reach the planchette easily on the board. "Okay. Everything's ready."

David sat at the end of the table and Albert and James on either side, facing one another.

James looked at everybody and smiled. "Albert, I hope you don't mind but David has always asked the questions. I mean. Well. It is HIS Ouija board."

Albert clapped his hands. "Sound good."

James smiled. "Now. You want to see something totally weird?" He turned the board over and pointed to the initials in the corner.

Albert looked at James and then David. "What's that?"

David continued. "When I bought the board, they were already there. Ishmael said I'd find out in time and Lorie had no clue about them. Yeah."

James turned the board back over and placed it on the table.

David spoke quietly. "Okay. Everyone put your fingers on the planchette. And no pushing." He sternly looked at James and Albert.

After a moment of silence, David spoke quietly. "Ishmael. Ishmael. Are you there?"

In no time at all, the planchette moved to 'YES'.

Everyone looked at each other and smiled.

"Ishmael. We're so sorry it's been so long since we contacted you. We do apologize."

The planchette began to move. 'NOT TO WORRY TIME IS IRRELEVANT TO ME'. There was a short pause and the planchette began to move again. 'WHAT MAY BE A HUNDRED YEARS TO YOU IS ONLY A MOMENT TO ME'.

Everyone had a surprised look on their faces.

Albert spoke very quietly. "Wow. That's really interesting."

David continued. "Ishmael. We have a question. Someone has joined James and me. He's told us he has used a Ouija board in the past and his guide's name was Ishmael. Is it possible you're the same, Ishmael?"

The planchette began to move. 'I AM LAUGHING'. After a moment, the planchette moved to 'YES HELLO ALBERT I AM SO GLAD YOU AND JAMES HAVE FOUND ONE ANOTHER'.

All were pleased with what they heard. "Wow." "Yeah." "Cool."

After their jubilation, David began again. "Ishmael. Do you have any additional information for us?"

The planchette started moving again. 'JUST REMEMBER THE DATE AND NUMBERS I GAVE YOU'. There was a pause. 'UNFORTUNATELY ALBERT CANNOT USE THESE NUMBERS AS IT WILL CONTAMINATE THE INTENT'.

David and James looked at Albert. David continued. "Ishmael, we understand. Albert understands. We know there's a reason but it doesn't matter."

'I AM GLAD YOU UNDERSTAND AS IT HAS NOTHING TO DO WITH ALBERT'. There was a pause. 'ALBERT IS A GOOD AND HONEST MAN BUT HE CANNOT CONTAMINATE THE INTENT'. Another pause. 'IF HE JOINS IN THE RESULTS WILL NOT HAPPEN AS THEY ARE INTENDED'.

Albert spoke quietly. "Not a problem. I sure as hell don't want to mess up a good thing. And I have a feeling it's a very good thing or Ishmael would never have told it to you."

The planchette began to move again. 'I SEE ALBERT UNDERSTANDS AND KNOWS IT IS NOT ANY REFLECTION ON HIM'.

David questioned. "So, you have no more information for us?"

The planchette moved to 'NO'.

"I do have one more question. The initials on the back of the board? Can you tell me anything more about them?"

The planchette moved. 'PATIENCE PATIENCE IN TIME YOU WILL UNDERSTAND BE PATIENT'.

"Ishmael. We want to thank you for all the information you've given us. We'll be touching bases with you in the future."

The planchette moved to 'NO'.

David questioned. "No?"

'CORRECT'.

"Why?"

'I HAVE SERVED MY PURPOSE AND GIVEN ALL OF YOU ALL THE INFORMATION YOU NEED TO KNOW FROM NOW ON FOR THE FUTURE THERE IS NO MORE INFORMATION I CAN GIVE YOU THAT WOULD BE OF ANY BENEFIT'. There was a pause, then the planchette began to move again. 'THE INFORMATION LORIE GAVE DAVID IS STILL OUTSTANDING I TELL YOU NOW THOSE THINGS WILL COME TO PASS'.

"Ishmael. We will miss you. We thank you for all you've given us."

'I HAVE ENJOYED OUR SESSIONS'. There was a slight pause. 'UNTIL WE MEET IN THE GREAT BEYOND I WISH ALL OF YOU WELL'. There was a pause. 'THIS IS MY LAST COMMENT TO ALL OF YOU'. There was one more pause. 'BE HAPPY AND TELL THOSE AROUND YOU THAT YOU LOVE THEM AND NEVER TAKE ANYONE FOR GRANTED'.

David commented. "Ishmael. I'll immediately try to find a place where someone may find this Ouija board and maybe you can help someone else down the road. You've been a great help to us. Thank you so very much."

The planchette moved again. 'EXCELLENT THAT IS AN EXCELLENT IDEA'.

They all called out. "Ishmael. Thank you and goodbye."

'GOODBYE MY FRIENDS HAVE A WONDERFUL LIFE TAKE CARE STAY HAPPY AND STAY WELL'. The planchette moved to 'GOOD BYE' at the bottom of the board.

There was total silence as all kept their fingers on the planchette for several moments, continuing to stare at the board. Slowly, they pulled their hands away and looked at one another.

James spoke very quietly. "Wow. Geez. I know this is going to sound crazy but I feel like I've just lost a really good friend."

Albert shook his head. "Yeah. I know what you mean. But you're right."

David looked down at the Ouija board and planchette. "I guess we'll not need this anymore. That's too bad. It was always so much fun."

Albert looked at David and James. "If you don't mind me asking, what is this about a date and numbers?"

David turned to Albert. "Way back in the very beginning, Ishmael gave us a date and a series of numbers, telling us not to forget them. They were very important. Interestingly enough, that same date was mentioned again by Lorie, the psychic reader, when we were Seniors in high school. So, we'll wait till that date arrives and hopefully realize what the numbers mean and take action."

James smiled and lifted his cocktail in the air. "To Ishmael. We thank you and we will miss you."

David and Albert raised their glasses, clinking them against James'.

All cried out. "To Ishmael! Hear! Hear! We will miss you."

CHAPTER V

There was silence in the room for a short period of time. Michael raised his hand. "James. Did you all ever try to contact Ishmael again?"

James shook his head. "No. We respected what Ishmael told us and we never brought out the Ouija board again. Actually, shortly thereafter, David gave it to one of those thrift shop places to see if they could get a few coins for it."

Michael sounded down. "Damn. This is going to sound incredibly stupid but I feel sad. He was an integral part of you all for fifteen years. Then. He was gone. Wow." He paused for a moment, smiled and raised his glass in the air. "Here's to Ishmael! Hear! Hear!"

Everyone in the room raised their glasses and cried out. "To Ishmael! Hear! Hear!"

Michael interrupted again. "Okay. Are we EVER going to know about the letters on the back of the Ouija board?"

James looked at Michael. "As Ishmael said. Patience. Patience."

Everyone clapped and cheered.

After everyone finally settled down again, James continued. "Now, let's jump forward a few years. It's now, nineteen eighty-one. Albert and I had bought this house and had been together for eight years. David was doing well and had bought a house of his own." He shook his head. "Now, he met and dated several guys during those years but none were the one for him. I believe in the back of his mind, remembering what Lorie told him, he knew if their names didn't start with an 'M' or 'F', there wasn't a chance they'd be the one. And NONE looked like some warrior hunter." He paused for a moment.

"It was the spring when David was called into the office of his boss. They'd finally put the puzzle together and realized David was gay. This didn't sit well with upper management and he was terminated. After that happened, we began to have concern for Albert. You all know the problems with many companies and their position on homosexuality. I always found it so interesting they would turn a blind eye when it came to adultery, hanky-panky and such by their employees. But oohh. Homosexuality was a definite firing offense. Yeah. We can't have those damn fucking queers around, giving the company a bad name. Fucking hypocrites. I was lucky. The company I work for isn't concerned about my sexuality. All they're interested in is my performance. They know I'm a superb employee and making the company a handsome sum every year."

Michael interrupted, waving his hand in the air. "Well. Finally. The filth mouth shows itself." He started laughing.

The room burst with laughter.

James shook his head. "What can I say? Thank you, Michael, for pointing that out."

The room roared with laughter again.

James smiled. "I shall continue. Yes. Things were getting better since Stonewall in nineteen sixty-nine but as you all know, there's still a long way to go. I wonder if I'll live long enough to see same-sex marriage legalized."

Michael raised his hand again and yelled out. "Yeah. Don't hold your breath on that one. You'd look like hell blue."

Sounds of agreement filled the room.

James smiled. "You've got that right!" He paused a moment. "Anyway, David wasn't deterred. His art was selling very well at galleries across the nation. In Roger's, too. He was constantly working on a commission as well as other canvases for the galleries."

"Finally, nineteen eighty-two rolled around. Now, remember that date and those numbers? Of course, you do. Well, it finally dawned on us. The numbers had to do with a lottery. Both of us could hardly wait."

"Eventually, November came and the week in question. David and I, both, flew to New York and we both bought a ticket with the specified numbers we were told by Ishmael. Yeah. We both had our fingers crossed to hear the results."

James and Albert invited David over for dinner the night of the twelfth. It was a Friday and no one had to work the next day. They fixed cocktails and started watching the TV. It was on the channel they knew the winning numbers for the multimillion-dollar lottery would be announced. James freshened everyone's drink and they sat down with bated breath. The hour of reckoning was at hand.

As the numbers appeared, James and David couldn't believe their eyes and ears. They held their breath. The last number was the power number. It was a… three.

They all looked at one another and after a moment of silence, they all jumped up and down, screaming and hugging one another. They couldn't believe it. Of course, it was possible more people had also picked the same numbers, reducing the winnings. But they didn't care. Any winnings would be wonderful.

As time passed, they discovered they were the only ones who had chosen all the numbers correctly. The total amount would be split two ways. James and Albert invited David over to explain the news.

"You do know. After taxes, we'll be getting only a little over four thousand dollars a week for twenty-five years." James couldn't help himself and began to roar with laughter. "Only four thousand dollars a week. Do you think we can make it on… four thousand dollars a week?"

All of them just burst out in raucous laughter over his sarcasm.

"James! With your genius, regarding stocks and investing, we can take a big chunk of that and make more. Not to sound greedy but it's true." David clapped his hands.

Albert called out. "You've got that right!"

James chuckled. "Four thousand dollars a week. Yeah. That's two hundred and eight thousand dollars a year. Not chicken feed. And that doesn't include any of the money we made after investing some of it. None of us had to work if we didn't want to."

"Yes. Even with that kind of money, we all decided we wanted to continue what we were doing. We all enjoyed it. David continued his painting, Albert stayed an engineer and I continued with the investment firm."

"I must tell you. With winning as you well know, our faces were plastered all over the news. Also, it became very obvious Albert and I were partners and we wondered about his engineering position. Interestingly enough, his firm was happy for him and had no problem with who he was. He was an excellent employee and did his job exceedingly well. Yep. David got fired but Albert and I didn't. As the old Meatloaf song goes. 'Two out of three ain't bad.'"

Clapping and cheers erupted from everyone.

"Okay, everyone. Do you remember what Lorie told David, regarding the ocean and a place where there were black volcanic rocks? Over the years, David had read quite a bit about Mexico. He even mentioned if he ever had the money, he'd love to get some property on the southwest coast and build a retirement home there. David loves the ocean. And why did he choose the southwest coast? Because there are very few hurricanes that make landfall there. Of course, there was the concern, regarding earthquakes but he felt he could deal with those much easier than the threat of hurricanes like the ones that pelt the eastern coast of the country."

"Not long after winning the lottery, he flew down to Zihuatanejo and looked for property there. He found a wonderful lot near the beach and the ocean, located about fifty miles up the coast from Zihuatanejo. He constantly refers to it as 'Beach in the Country'. It's so far out in the boonies."

"Yep. He got a lot, found a builder and began construction. And yes. David designed his own house. It took a little over a year to complete. So, you see? Lorie was correct. Black volcanic rock juts from the ocean and the beach in that area. They use it as their home base."

"Now. Let me see. I believe it was just over six years ago, not long after the completion of the Mexico house when David got a wild hair. He wanted a change of scenery. He wanted new ideas for his paintings."

"Yes. He had the beauty of the southwest coast of Mexico with the crashing waves on the rocks and beach but David always said the ocean is one of the most difficult things to paint. He'd done several but wasn't totally pleased with the way they turned out." James smiled. "I believe if you saw those paintings, you wouldn't have any problem, hanging them on your walls."

Michael raised his hand. "Hey! If any of you've seen David's work, you know full well he's no slouch when it comes to slinging paint with a brush." He paused for a moment. "And we have another incredible artist with us tonight who's no slouch with a brush. Richard. Yeah." He pointed to one of the guests. "Go to Roger's gallery and check out his work. You'll see what I mean." He started clapping his hands

This had the whole group cheering and clapping.

James shook his head in the affirmative. "Michael. I absolutely agree with you. David is his own worst critic. So is Richard. Sometimes I'd like to slap them both upside the head."

This comment made everyone chuckle.

"But let me continue." He paused a moment. "Checking out travel magazines, he came across some pictures of the mountains and forests in South America. He believed seeing the area and taking photographs would give him a huge selection for a great number of new paintings."

"To get into the thick of things, he did some extensive research and came across a place in the central section of South America in northern Brazil. He'd use the town as a jumping-off place for his expeditions into the wild. The name of the town is Barcelos."

"Yep. Barcelos. Located on the Rio Negro. A river in northern Brazil. It took two years to arrange but with a little digging and checking, he planned to have a boat chartered that could take him up the river and into tributaries. He also hired a guide, Ricardo, who was recommended by the hotel in the town. The person with whom he chartered the boat indicated he and his crew would have no problem, taking him to the natural parts of the river, taking care of having enough supplies and food for the trips while he did all his photography. The boat pilot knew the guide David had hired and they'd work well together."

"One thing he wanted to do when he first arrived was to take a helicopter ride around and over the area, so he could check out possible locations where he could take pictures. Again, the pilot was recommended by the hotel in Barcelos as being reliable, responsible and reasonable in price. His name is Miguel. It was all set. David was going to be gone for two months."

"It wasn't until four years ago in August of nineteen eighty-five, everything was finalized and he was off and on the way with his journey."

David got off the small charter plane and looked around. He then looked up toward the sun and muttered. "I sure am glad I brought a couple of hats to wear down here. That sun would burn the hell out of the top of my head." He was referring to the loss of his hair by age twenty-eight.

It was Monday the fifth, the beginning of the second week in the month. He smiled and was very excited about his new adventure. The weather was quite warm. This was just the start. Much traveling would have to be done to reach major locations where he wanted to take pictures. There would be many incredible shots along the way. This whole area of the Amazon was riddled with potentially amazing photos. He was so glad he'd packed over a hundred rolls of thirty-five millimeter film for his camera. Yeah. Each roll had thirty-six exposures. He knew finding more film could be a real problem, so he wanted to come prepared.

Just then, he saw a tall, handsome, well-built man, dark brown hair, beard and mustache, wearing a brimmed hat, walking toward him with a big smile on his face. He looked to be around his own age. He didn't have the facial characteristics of those Hispanics of Mexico and South America. His features were more European and Castilian.

The man extended his right hand. "Hello. You must be Señor David. Welcome to Barcelos. I am Ricardo, your guide." They shook hands. "Let us get your things and we will go to your hotel and you can get settled."

"Ricardo. Thank you very much. And please. No Señor. Call me David."

They gathered all of David's things and headed to the hotel.

After signing in, the desk clerk told David the bellboy would take his things to the room. It was right next to the one he'd arranged for Ricardo. David smiled. "Thank you very much. Please, give this to the bellboy when he returns." He handed the clerk some currency, having about the value of a dollar. "Do you have a safe here for your guests?"

"Yes, Señor David." The clerk smiled.

"I'd gratefully appreciate you keeping this in your safe. I may need it to pay those helping me. Señor Ricardo here will have access to this money as well. There may be others I'll tell you about. Please, tell others who work here of my request. This is in case, I'm not in a position to get it myself." He snickered. "Hey. You never know. I might be abducted by aliens. What can I say?"

Everyone laughed.

David pulled out a very large sum of money in large denomination bills of the country and counted them in front of the clerk.

"Señor David. That is a very large amount of money. Are you sure you do not want to take it to the local bank? They can hold it for you as well." The clerk was concerned over the large amount.

"You know. That's a good idea. I'll change some of this into smaller denominations to use around. I'm sure most folks don't have change for large bills like these. I'll leave some here and put the major portion in the bank. Thank you for the suggestion." He counted out a sum he wanted the hotel to hold and gave it to the clerk who wrote out a receipt for him. He thanked the clerk and turned to Ricardo. "We can get something to eat then head to the bank. Now. Let's go into the restaurant and have a drink. We can go over some tentative plans for the time I'm going to be here."

Ricardo smiled. "Right this way." He gestured in the direction of the restaurant. "And thank you so very much for allowing me to stay here in the hotel with you. It will definitely save the time it would take me to come from my house. I also appreciate you giving me permission to have access to your money. That is extremely generous of you."

"Well. Seriously. You never know." David grinned. "Hey. With you staying here, will allow us to discuss things during our downtime when we're not out in the countryside. By the way, if it wasn't clear, I was hoping we'd eat together, so we can talk about things. Remember. This trip is on me and I want you to be comfortable as well. Anything you order, put it on your room tab. Not a problem."

"David. Thank you so much. I do appreciate it." He gave a big smile.

The restaurant host led them to a table. Sitting down at the table, David removed his hat and placed it on an adjacent chair. He looked at Ricardo and smiled. "With all that wonderful dark hair, you don't have to worry about the top of your head getting sunburned like I do."

Ricardo removed his hat as well. He smiled. "I still have to wear a hat when I go out in the sun. Dark hair warms up very quickly here."

A few minutes passed before a waiter came over and took their order. Ricardo was extremely helpful in interpreting the menu. David gave the waiter his room number. The waiter smiled as he left the table.

"I'll tell the front desk any charges on your room will be paid by me. I wasn't sure if that was clear to them."

"Ricardo. It's nice to meet you. I'm really looking forward to this adventure. I believe I'll be able to take enough photographs they could possibly keep me busy painting for the rest of my life." David was curious. "By the way, your English is excellent. How is it you learned it so well way out here in the boonies?"

Ricardo stroked his beard with his left hand. "Well. I must be honest. I did my education in Rio de Janeiro and learned my English there."

"Okay. I give up. If you did your studies in Rio, what the hell are you doing way out here in no man's land?" David's face was filled with question.

Ricardo smiled. "I love the outdoors. I love the wilderness. I heard about this place and wanted to check it out. After seeing all the beauty in the area, I realized that slowly, this place would become a destination for visitors who wanted to experience nature and the wilds. I knew any tourists coming here would most likely want and need a guide to take them to spots of interest. So, here I am."

David agreed. "Well, you definitely have that right. In checking out places to stay here, I found your name mentioned by all of them as an excellent guide."

Ricardo had a questioning look on his face. "Okay. My turn. How on earth did you discover Barcelos? After all, it presently is not one of South America's major tourist centers."

David just grinned and shook his head. "Yes. I know. But I wanted a place untouched by civilization. In my research, this place came up. Now, I'm not trying to be ugly as I realize this town used to be the capital of Amazonas from seventeen twenty-eight to seventeen fifty-eight. But it IS located in an area off the beaten track for the typical tourist. I believe I'll be able to take pictures here and do paintings from them, showing the beauty and wonders here. Who knows? Folks may see my paintings and want to check this area of the world out."

Ricardo nodded his head. "You are correct. This is not a typical place tourists would normally choose to come to. Just as I said. Only those seeking the wilderness and the wilds. The scenery here is absolutely beautiful. Wait until you see the waterfalls. Any pictures you have seen truly do not do them justice. When we go on your helicopter ride tomorrow, I will direct the pilot, Miguel, to areas I believe you will find exceptional for photography. By the way, so you know. Miguel is very good and does speak English. Also, his helicopter is a Bell 206B Jet Ranger. He modified the tank, so he would get around six hundred miles when full. This allows him to do extended flying in virtually any area his customers might want to go."

"That'll be perfect. Thank you. I just knew you were going to be a gigantic help in this venture. There's one area rather out of the way, I'd like to see. I understand there's a tributary, going north off the Rio Negro and up into a mountainous area. I think it's called the Rio Demini."

"Yes. I know the area of which you speak. It is the Rio Demini. Also, the Rio Araçà goes north from that waterway. It is a place rarely gone to since it is so far away. I have been up that way only twice. It is very remote. But I have not gone very far up the Rio Araçà or as far as the major mountainous area. Virtually no one has wanted to take the time to venture up that way when they come here. Probably due to their time constraint of a two-week vacation. But with you having two months, there should be plenty of time. If you really want to go in that direction, I would allow at least three to four weeks for that trip because the river is very winding and cannot be traversed quickly. If you like, we can do a quick sweep of that whole area in the helicopter and you can see places you might like to photograph."

"Since you know of the waterways going there, maybe it would be a good idea for us to fly over that area tomorrow. I'm looking forward to the entire trip tomorrow. I think it'll be extremely informative."

Ricardo smiled. "Excellent. And again, I really do appreciate it that you arranged for me to stay here in the hotel." He paused for a moment. "The helicopter is to be here at nine tomorrow morning. Of course, weather permitting." Ricardo gave a big grin. "I highly recommend you get rested and organize all your equipment if you want to take any on the helicopter ride."

"Actually, I'm not going to take any photographs from the helicopter. I just want to see the areas of interest and where they're located in relationship to the town here."

Ricardo continued. "Your boat will be at the dock next Monday at around nine in the morning. They will already have all the supplies necessary for any extended trips. I know you had considered using tents for extended trips out into the jungle or on the river but I tell you. It is much better we stay on the boat or return here to the hotel at night. There are many creatures of the night out there and it could be quite dangerous if we stayed in tents."

"I have already talked to the pilot of the boat, indicating places I am sure you would like to see, so he can chart his course. When I see him on Monday, I will tell him of the trip you want to take up north into the mountains. After our helicopter ride tomorrow, if you see any other locations along the waterways, let me know and I can alert the boat pilot." Ricardo smiled. "I believe you are in for a very fun and interesting time here. I do not think you will be disappointed."

CHAPTER VI

The helicopter trip the next day was extremely informative. Ricardo was correct. The areas he'd chosen for David to see were exactly what David was looking for. The trip over the mountainous area north of Barcelos was very helpful. David was glad they did it. He could see several areas of interest. There was one smaller tributary, heading north off of the Rio Araçà. It went right north into a valley between two mountainous areas. Ricardo indicated it would probably take a smaller boat to go up that waterway. This wasn't a problem. A small motorboat was always brought along on the boat he'd hired.

The next several days, Ricardo led David to a few places within walking and hiking distance of the hotel. The scenery was amazing. There were still other places Ricardo wanted to take David but would be done at another time.

One accessory David had brought with him was a set of six walkie-talkies. He also brought a very large supply of batteries to keep them working. He was told they could reach a distance of at least a mile and maybe more if there were no major objects between them.

The next Monday morning, Ricardo helped David bring his

supplies and equipment to the dock. There he met the boat pilot, Juan. It was obvious Ricardo would be his interpreter go-between with Juan and his three-member crew. Ricardo explained to Juan that David wanted to take an extended trip up the tributaries into the mountains north of the Rio Negro. This trip would probably take as long as three or four weeks and he should plan on four. Juan indicated it would be no problem. He'd never taken the boat up that far, so it would be a new adventure for him as well.

For two weeks, the boat trip went up the Rio Negro and back, stopping several times along the way. Ricardo would lead David into the jungle to show him several sites of interest.

David couldn't believe it. Every shot he took was a potential canvas. Some of the flowering plants were so spectacular, he began to joke. "Too bad Georgia O'Keeffe's not here to paint them."

When the boat returned to Barcelos, David informed the boat pilot he wouldn't need him for two weeks but to come back on Monday, September ninth for the next trip, heading up into the mountains to the north.

Ricardo wanted to take David hiking to the west and south of Barcelos. He also wanted to take him to see some of the local waterfalls.

One evening while they were having dinner and drinks, David joked. "Ricardo. I love these day trips but I swear they wear me out. This much exercise is killing me."

Ricardo just grinned. "But it is good for you."

"Yeah. Sure. Believe it." David took a drink of his cocktail. "I have to admit, I've never seen such natural beauty before stashed all in one area. I can hardly wait to get back home and start painting again."

"When you do, you will have to send some pictures of some of your paintings, so I can see them."

"I will. I definitely will."

Yes. David was totally amazed at the jungle scenery and the waterfalls. Every day made him more and more pleased he was on this adventure.

James looked around the room. "Okay, everyone. I believe this is a good spot to take a short break. Run to the bathroom, get more munchies and refill your drinks. We'll continue shortly."

Soon, everyone was back at their seats and James continued. "Yes. David's next boat trip was going to be amazing. But something would happen none of them expected. It would seem David's desire to reach the mountainous area would be dashed. But David was to discover something about Ricardo truly unexpected."

Over the two weeks, David and Ricardo made day trips into the jungle from the hotel, they'd share their meals together and began to get to know one another. After dinner one evening, conversation began to get more personal. They both had consumed several cocktails while they relaxed in the hotel restaurant.

Ricardo shook his head. "You know. I look back at my life so far and all I can do is shake my head. When I was in school in Rio de Janeiro, I had a boyfriend who was..." His drinking had let his guard slip. He stopped short and looked directly at David with shock and embarrassment on his face, hoping he might not have heard. "I mean. Ah."

David smiled and looked directly at Ricardo. "Ricardo. Yes. I heard what you said. But not to worry. I've had several boyfriends in my life."

They both looked at one another and after a moment of silence, bent their heads down and started snickering.

David commented. "No wonder you're such a terrific guide. Let me tell you. We gay guys are the absolute best when it comes to the servicing industries. I'll also tell you, you've given no hint at all of your orientation. No one would ever know unless you told them."

Ricardo gave a sigh of relief. "David. I try not to let people know. It is not easy for gay people in the world today. If they find out, no one will hire you. They instantly think you are a pedophile or worse."

David spoke with conviction. "Hey. You're preaching to the choir. I got sacked from my job four years ago when they found out. I totally understand what you're saying." He paused for a moment then changed the subject. "Ricardo. You're a very good-looking man. From the time I've spent with you so far, it's obvious you have a wonderful personality as well. Don't you get lonely way out here in the wilderness?"

Ricardo responded. "Once in a while, I take a little vacation down to Rio and have a good time while I am there. I have yet to meet anyone who could be of possible significance. And it is okay. I do not mind being single. And you have to be so careful with the AIDs epidemic going on."

"Yes. I know exactly what you mean. Also, I haven't met anyone special, either. Although..." David bent his head down and paused for a moment. "You may not believe this and think I'm crazy but a psychic lady once told me I'd eventually meet someone whose name started with an 'M' or 'F'. Yeah. What's also really weird is this guy is living with people who have darker skin than his and resemble the Indians, living out west in the United States. I've yet to take a trip out to any of the Indian reservations to check this out. What can I say?" He paused again. "There's also a carved stone snake near water associated with him. Yeah."

Ricardo's face was filled with surprise. "Really? You believe in that kind of stuff? Do I dare tell you, I do, too? But I have never had the guts to go to a fortune teller or psychic reader. I know there are good ones out there but so many of them are fake. I am so afraid I will pick one of the fake ones."

David knew he had to tell Ricardo. "Well, since you've opened the door, have I got a story to tell you."

For the next almost two hours, David told the story of James and himself through the years. Ricardo was totally surprised by Ishmael's predictions coming true. What really shocked him was the winning of the lottery, using the information Ishmael had given them.

"Well. On one of your extended vacations, you're going to have to come to Atlanta and meet many of my friends. Who knows? You just might meet someone very special there." David gave a big smile.

Ricardo slapped his hand on the table. "Hey. You never know."

Now. Since the ice had been broken and as time progressed, David and Ricardo began to share more of their personal lives. It brought them even closer together as friends.

"By the way, they have Ricardo visiting and will be coming with them tonight. So, you're also going to be able to meet Ricardo." James smiled.

Michael raised his hand. "Yeah. I remember seeing Ricardo on that TV special Donald did. He's one very good-looking and sexy man. James. Is he still single?"

James just nodded. "Michael. From what I understand, yes, Ricardo is single. I believe if he had someone of significance, that person would've come along as well. You can find out for yourself when you meet him later on when they get here."

Michael flexed his eyebrows several times and a huge grin came to his face. "Yeah. And he speaks English, too. Whaa Hoo!"

Laughter filled the room.

David and Ricardo gathered everything they planned to take with them on the trip up the rivers. They also made arrangements with the hotel and Miguel. If they weren't back in four weeks to come looking for them. Ricardo thought it a very good plan in case of an emergency since radio communication was virtually nonexistent in that area. They'd use the walkie-talkies to communicate while away from the boat, taking pictures.

Heading up the Rio Demini, David was amazed at how spectacular the scenery was. It was the same, going up the Rio Araçá. This river had many, many, winding curves in it and had to be negotiated very carefully. Juan had never brought the boat this far north on the river. Ricardo had never been this far, either.

They finally reached a section that was very shallow and questionable if the boat could get through it. This location was still far from where David wanted his final destination to be.

The decision was made to turn the boat around and head back to Barcelos. David felt some disappointment but he'd taken many wonderful pictures along the way.

Ricardo clapped his hands together and smiled. "When we get back to Barcelos, you can hire Miguel to take us up to where you want to go. I am sure he would be able to find at least one location to land."

"Ricardo! That's an excellent idea. I don't know why I didn't think of it." David did the Snoopy Happy Dance. "I just might get my mountainous photographs after all."

The area David wanted to check out was virtually a hundred and thirty to a hundred and fifty miles as the crow flies directly north of Barcelos. The helicopter could make that trip in no time at all compared to the boat, having to wind all around the curves in the rivers.

Ricardo continued. "We can fly up into that area, spend a couple of days then fly back to Barcelos. This would mean we do not have to rough it for any extended period of time."

"I love it!" David was ecstatic at Ricardo's suggestion. "That being the case, I'm going to make it possible for Miguel to have access to the cash at the hotel and bank just as I did with you. It'll give him the money he'll need for fuel and any other expenses he might incur related to my need for his services. We can take care of that when we get back to Barcelos. I can also have my bank in Atlanta wire more money to this bank down here."

The minute they arrived in Barcelos, Ricardo made arrangements with Miguel. It would be no problem. They could carry enough easy food, water, toiletries and sleeping bags to spend like two or three days before returning.

David thanked Juan and his crew for all they'd done and paid them the full amount they'd have received for the entire trip upriver. Juan was very thankful and told David he'd be of service to him in the future should the occasion ever arise.

It was also obvious to David, he was going to be on vacation longer than the original two months he'd planned. He made arrangements with the hotel for him and Ricardo to stay longer into October. He also made arrangements for Miguel to stay there. This wouldn't be a problem. He also notified the private plane that brought him to Barcelos. He wouldn't be leaving as he originally planned. He told them he'd give them notice when to come get him. Again, this wasn't going to be a problem. He also notified close friends in Atlanta of his decision to stay longer. All they had to say was. "Have a good time."

Miguel picked them up on Monday, September thirtieth. They flew up early, so it would give them time to peruse the area for potential landing sites. Miguel was actually surprised. There were several areas where he indicated would be no problem landing the helicopter. Finding this out, David picked the first place he'd like to come to on the next trip.

At dinner that night in the restaurant, David, Ricardo and Miguel discussed the possibilities of the next day.

"That whole area up there is so beautiful. I'm sure I'll be able to get numerous photographs of the mountains." David was overjoyed. "Ricardo. I do appreciate you letting me keep you longer than I'd intended." He turned to Miguel. "I also appreciate you letting me hire you again on such short notice. And both of you remember. If you need any money to cover expenses, go to the hotel clerk or the bank. They know you both and it will be no problem."

Miguel smiled. "Not a problem. I will not be doing any booking until you have no more need of me. And that is very generous of you, regarding the money."

Ricardo commented. "That is definitely not a problem. And as for the trip to the mountains, I am glad you will be able to get the pictures you wanted. Now, some of those landing sites are pretty high. We will have to hike down to the valleys to get any pictures from there while Miguel stays with the helicopter."

"Hey! With all the walking I've done so far on this trip, I feel like I could run a marathon." David thrust his fist into the air as he yelled out. "YeeeHaw!"

The phone rang. Albert went and answered it. "Not a problem. Take your time. No one's going anywhere. They're all having a great time. We'll see you when you get here." He turned to James. "James. That was David. He said he apologized but they're running late. He hoped you didn't mind."

James just smiled. "Well. That does give me more time to continue with the story. Also, fill your plates and refresh your drinks. I'll continue in a few."

After everyone got and did what they needed, they again got settled and waited for James to go forward with his story.

"Yes. On that first trip to the mountains, the helicopter landed on a plateau. This gave David a spectacular view of the valley below and the mountain range to the east."

"It was perfect for them to spend three days there and venture into the valley below. This was the valley between the mountain ranges, containing the tributary they'd planned to traverse in the motorboat."

"In those three days, David took many pictures. Several taken were of an incredible sunset on the evening of the first day they were there. David joked it reminded him of some of the paintings he'd seen by J. M. W. Turner, the nineteenth century English artist."

"When they flew back to Barcelos, Miguel indicated he wanted to batten down the helicopter until they were ready to go again. He also wanted them to fill the tank. He'd join them later at the hotel."

"The next two days, all three just sat around, relaxing and discussing the next trip to the mountains. On this next trip, they'd land in the mountains east of the valley they saw on their last trip. They decided to stay another three days."

"Little did any of them realize. This upcoming trip was going to be significantly anything but ordinary. An event was going to occur, changing David's life forever."

CHAPTER VII

It was Sunday, October sixth when they flew up to the mountains again. When they reached the area, David wanted to pick out a location to land on the east side of the valley. Miguel remembered a location, centrally located and fairly high on a ridge.

David smiled as they landed. "Miguel. This is great. Ricardo and I can hike down toward the valley from here and check out the whole area." He climbed out of the helicopter, got his camera and started taking photographs. Some toward the west and then toward the east. The views were spectacular from where they had landed.

Ricardo and David hiked down into the valley for more photographs. As the sun began to set, David got some amazing photos, looking toward the west. The sky was filled with color.

As night set in, David mentioned the next day he'd like to climb up onto one of the highest ridges to get a panoramic view. Ricardo indicated they'd most likely be heading north to reach some of the highest points.

"Ricardo. I have to tell you. I'm so pleased with how this entire vacation has gone. Even though we couldn't reach this area by boat, I'm still glad we took the boat trip. It was leisurely and quite a bit of fun."

Ricardo smiled. "I am so glad you are not disappointed. I am sure Miguel feels the same way. We like our clients to be happy and satisfied."

"Do you think we'll have much trouble, reaching a high place tomorrow?" David scratched his beard with his right hand.

"I think if we take our time we can probably reach a spot where we can see almost forever in all directions." Ricardo responded.

Suddenly, David jumped up, put his right hand on his chest and stretched the left arm up and out, breaking into song. "'On a clear day, you can see forever. On a clear day, you can see forever. And on a clear day, you can see forever, and ever, and ever, and evermore.'" He paused for a moment and smiled. "My apologies to Barbra Streisand."

They all broke out in loud laughter.

David could hardly sleep that night, pondering the sites he might see the next day. He knew he had to sleep, so he'd be rested for the next day's hiking.

Miguel was up early, fixing coffee on the campfire. "Is anyone hungry? I can fix some eggs and bacon from the cooler."

Ricardo answered. "Just coffee for me. I will eat something when we get back."

David spoke. "Same for me. But if you're hungry, fix yourself something. I don't want anybody to be hungry."

After having their coffee, David and Ricardo took one of the walkie-talkies and told Miguel if they had any problems, they'd contact him. David strapped his camera over his shoulder and Ricardo grabbed the pair of binoculars. Then, they were off.

It took them over four hours to carefully climb to one of the highest points in the area. David was totally amazed at the view. "Ricardo. You're right. From here, you CAN almost see forever."

Ricardo shook his head. "I regret I have never been up this way. The views from up here are spectacular. Now, knowing I can get here by helicopter, I will have to suggest to my future clients to come up here for at least a day trip."

David took several pictures facing east. Then, he turned west and took more of the mountain range on the other side of the valley. He turned to his left, taking some shots to the southwest. He then faced directly west and took several shots. Lastly, he turned in a northwesterly direction and began taking several shots.

As he was focusing his camera for the last picture in that direction, something caught his eye. He noticed a strange anomaly on the far, lower, northeast cliff of the far mountain. It was facing directly east.

"Ricardo? There's something strange on the face of that far cliff." He pointed in the direction to where he was referring. "I can't quite make it out. But?" He began to chuckle. "My instant first impression was something built into the side of the mountain. Are there tribal people, living up in this area? Could it be like the cliff dwellers of the western United States?"

Ricardo raised his binoculars and looked in the direction David had pointed. "I do not know of any people living in this area. Maybe it is the ruins of some ancient culture." He focused the binoculars and looked at the cliff face. "Wow! David, you are right! It does look like ruins. This could be an historic discovery."

"How about we fly over there and see if Miguel can find a landing place close enough for us to hike down and check it out?" David was ecstatic.

Ricardo got on the walkie-talkie. "Miguel. Put out the campfire and get ready to leave. David and I have discovered something very unusual on the far western mountain range. We want to fly over there and check it out."

They immediately began their trek back to the helicopter. During their hike, they began to discuss and ponder what they'd seen.

It was late afternoon when they reached the helicopter. Miguel had seen them coming and started the engine. Right after liftoff, Miguel took the helicopter in the direction David pointed.

"Over there! It's on the east face of that far mountain. Before we go for a landing site, I'd like for us to go and get as close as possible to it. I can take a few pictures of it from the air." David was excited.

Within a very short time, Miguel had the helicopter hovering just above the trees and some five hundred feet from the face of the cliff. All were amazed at what they saw. They were just far enough away. The scene fit totally in the several pictures David shot.

Ricardo spoke quietly. "This is fantastic. We may have stumbled upon an ancient historic site. I cannot wait until we get down there and do some exploring."

David agreed. "I can't believe we've come across this. It reminds me of the ancient cliff dwellers discovered in the western part of the United States."

Ricardo shook his head. "I can understand why this may not have been discovered before. It truly is out in the middle of nowhere. As much time as I have spent in Barcelos even knowing the beauty of these mountains, I have never done any exploring up in this region. It is so far out of the way from everything."

"Well. What do you think? The opening looks like it's about two hundred feet wide and maybe fifty or sixty feet high at the highest point?" David clicked another picture.

Ricardo shook his head in the affirmative. "That sounds about right. I wonder how old it is. I am surprised at what good shape it looks to be in. I think we will be able to tell more when we can get up close and check it out." Ricardo continued to stare at the stone structures built inside the cavity of the cliff.

"Maybe it's not ancient. Maybe it's more recent than we think." David's face took on a questioning look. "Miguel. Can we fly closer and hover for a few minutes, so we can get a better look at the structures?"

Miguel responded. "Not a problem." He maneuvered the helicopter to within about fifty feet in front of the dwellings. They held there for almost ten minutes.

David was ecstatic. "We can go set up camp for the night then hike down here and check things out. Yeah."

Miguel directed the helicopter up and started searching for a safe landing site as close as possible to the find. Everyone had their eyes peeled for a possible location.

Miguel cried out. "Ah. I see one. But it looks like it may take you a couple of hours to hike down to the valley."

Ricardo suggested. "Since it is so late, I think we should camp out for the night and go down early in the morning."

"Great idea." David agreed.

It only took Miguel a few minutes to land. They took their time organizing a campsite and getting ready to hunker down for the night. The new discovery dominated their conversation the whole evening. They all wondered what kind of impact this would have on the history of Brazil as well as South America.

David found it very difficult to sleep, wondering what the next day would bring. He spoke quietly to himself. "I can't believe this is really happening to me." He knew he had to get rest. There was no telling what would be happening the next day.

To David, it seemed he'd just closed his eyes and fallen asleep when he realized it was time to get up. He yawned and stretched his arms in the air. "Damn! Is it morning already? I feel like I just went to sleep."

Ricardo scratched his beard. "I know what you mean. Seems Miguel got up first." He looked over at Miguel who was sitting by the fire.

Miguel was up early, fixing coffee, bacon and eggs. Not only was he a great helicopter pilot but a pretty good cook, too.

David drank some of his coffee then spoke. "Ricardo. You and Miguel are going to be in history books, having discovered a new civilization in South America."

Miguel smiled. "It should be interesting to find out what archaeologists will have to say about the site."

Ricardo drank the last of his coffee. "Okay. We need to get moving. Time is not standing still."

It took Ricardo and David nearly three hours to hike down to the floor of the valley and get into position in front of the stone constructions built inside the cavity in the side of the cliff. They moved back as far from the cliff as possible for David to take his photographs. The stone dwellings were about sixty feet from the floor of the valley.

David was jubilant. "Ricardo! This is incredible! My photographs will never do it justice."

Ricardo got on the walkie-talkie. "Miguel. I wish you could see this. It is amazing. I have a feeling we are the first outsiders to ever see it. Yeah. We will keep you posted. Later." He began to examine the side of the cliff below the structures. "How does anyone get up there? I do not see any steps or footholds to do it."

"Well. I'm sure whoever lived there had some way of getting up. There are no obvious means probably for defense reasons. Guess they just didn't want any Tom, Dick or Harry dropping in unexpectedly." David snickered as he continued to examine the face of the cliff.

"Very funny." Ricardo shook his head. "I would like to get up there and check things out. To see a discovery, no one else has ever seen before would be incredible. I know if we can get up there, not to touch or move anything. Archaeologists would have a fit if we did."

David shouted. "Rope ladders!"

"Rope ladders?" Ricardo tilted his head in questioning. After a split second, he understood. "Of course! Rope ladders! That is how they would get up and down. With the ladders pulled up, no uninvited guests would come to visit. You have that right."

Ricardo looked up toward the structures and shook his head. "I do not know what to say. I have no idea how we can get up there. It is a shame to have come all this way and not be able to do it."

David seemed disappointed. "Yes. I know what you mean. But we have no equipment with us right now to get up there. If we only had a grappling hook and rope, we could do it. We'll have to bring one on our next trip here."

Ricardo got on the walkie-talkie again. "Miguel. We are going to head back up to you since there is no way we can reach the structures. We can fly back to Barcelos and come back tomorrow with some rope and things, so we can climb up there. See you in a couple of hours."

David and Ricardo stood there, peering up at the structures before they were to leave.

David chuckled. "'Afta all. Tamara IS anotha day.'" He began to laugh harder.

Ricardo turned, looking at David. "I know there is supposed to be something funny with what you said and how you said it but I do not get it."

David shook his head. "It's a quote from an old movie. A true classic. Not to worry. I'll explain it later."

Ricardo smiled. "Okay."

Just as they were about to turn and hike back up to the helicopter, they heard a sound, coming from behind and to their left. They both turned to see what it was.

There, standing at the edge of the undergrowth, were several indigenous men. They were dressed only in hide loincloths, moccasin shoes and carrying spears. The indigenous men had black, straight hair, no body or facial hair and their skin was a dark brown. They uttered not a sound but had questioning expressions on their faces.

What shocked David and Ricardo was the man, standing in front of them, leading the group. He was tall, well-built, wearing the same apparel as the natives and also carrying a spear. But. His hair was brown and slightly curly. He had a beard and mustache. His skin was light in color. Brown hair covered his chest, stomach, forearms and legs. He, too, spoke not a word but the expression on his face was one of wondering.

David looked right into the man's face. He couldn't believe it. The man had amazing, jade green eyes. Suddenly, he remembered what Lorie had said those many years ago about a jade green color being associated with the man. "Oh! My! God! What have we stumbled upon?" He slowly turned to Ricardo. "I'm not sure but I think we may be in real trouble here."

CHAPTER VIII

Ricardo slowly reached and got his walkie-talkie. "Miguel. Miguel. I think we are in trouble. There are native people here with spears. Yes. That is right. Spears. David and I are not moving. No quick movements. If you do not hear back from us soon, head back to Barcelos and let authorities know. Over and out." He slowly placed his walkie-talkie back on his belt.

David spoke quietly. "Something's wrong with this picture." He paused for a moment and then spoke quietly with surprise. "It's what Lorie told me a million years ago. What she said has come true. She mentioned jade green. Look at his eyes. They're a jade green color. She couldn't imagine a light-skinned man alongside those of a native tribe. But. Here he is. I assumed she was talking about some Indian tribe in the western United States. But I was wrong. He is here."

A strange and questioning expression came to the face of the tall, brown-haired man. Everyone in his party stayed in place while he took several steps forward. In a quiet yet concerned voice, he spoke very slowly. "How is it... you speak... my... secret language?"

David's mouth fell open in shock. He was so stunned, it took him several moments to speak. He blurted out. "Ah! Ah! Oh, my God! You speak English! How is it you speak English!?"

The man tilted his head in question. "No." He spoke very slowly. "You are speaking... my secret language. I did not know others knew my secret language."

Ricardo spoke quietly. "THIS is really bizarre. Not only does he look out of sync with the group but he is speaking English. Wow. Talk about something being totally off-the-wall as you would say."

David smiled and spoke slowly. "My name is David." He used his right hand, pointing at himself. This is Ricardo." He gestured in Ricardo's direction with his right hand.

The man smiled. "My name is Muraroot." He pointed at himself with his left hand. "These are my friends." He gestured to those standing behind him. "We have never seen outsiders come here before. Why are you here and where do you come from?"

David shook his head. "I'll tell you but I can see there's much to understand here. Ricardo needs to let Miguel know we're all right."

Ricardo grabbed his walkie-talkie. "Miguel. It seems things are calm right now. It is obvious there is much to find out here. I will keep you posted. You are NOT going to believe this."

Muraroot spoke softly. "I think we have much to talk about. Let us go to a place where we can sit down." He pointed to the face of the cliff. Turning to his friends, he spoke to them in their language, explaining their intentions.

Everyone walked to the wall of the cliff. One man tilted his head back, cupped his hands around his mouth and let out a loud yodeling cry. After a few minutes, a rope ladder came rolling down the face of the cliff.

Muraroot turned to David. "We go." He started climbing the ladder followed by David and Ricardo then by the rest of the men.

When they reached the top, David turned to Muraroot and asked. "Do you mind if I take pictures? I have a camera here." He held it up for Muraroot to see.

Muraroot looked at the camera. "Will it hurt anyone when you take pictures?"

David smiled. "No. It won't hurt anyone." He began taking pictures.

Slowly, they walked through the stone dwellings and deeper into the cavern. David and Ricardo had no idea how extensive and deep the cavern was. It had to extend at least three hundred feet into the mountain and contained a vast number of structures.

Walking along, David noticed something. "Ricardo. I don't see any people but I know they're there. Not a sound, either."

Ricardo looked around. "Even the guys behind us are disappearing. I guess they're no longer needed."

At the back of the cavern was a cave about four hundred feet long, leading to an opening on the other side. There was a large cavity on that side as well, containing numerous stone structures. It looked out onto a small valley encircled by mountains.

Ricardo commented. "I do not think I can reach Miguel from here. I will have to go back to the other side to do that."

"You just might have to do that later on. Something tells me we're going to be in a rather lengthy discussion with Muraroot. There has to be some explanation as to how he got here since he obviously doesn't belong." David's mind kept trying to figure it out.

Muraroot turned to David. "We will go to my father's house and talk." He led them to one of the stone dwellings. "My father is the leader of the tribe." By this time, all the other men had left the group.

David and Ricardo looked at one another with a shocked expression, hearing that Muraroot's father was there.

David spoke softly. "There are more light-skinned people here? Really?" He was completely confused. None of this made any sense.

As they walked into the dwelling, David and Ricardo saw several native men, sitting at a table. None had light skin. All the men stood up when they saw them enter.

Muraroot walked over to one of the men. "This is my father."

Ricardo and David looked at one another with a shocked expression. This made no sense at all.

David shook his head. "Muraroot. I don't understand. You say this man is your father. You have light skin. Your father has darker skin. How is this possible?"

"My father knows the whole story. He will help me tell it to you.

I need to tell him about you. He has never seen outsiders." Muraroot explained. "Everyone sit down."

Two of the native men gave David and Ricardo their seats. All sat down.

David explained to Muraroot who he and Ricardo were. He also told them why they were in the area. They'd seen the stone dwellings from the other side of the valley and wanted to check it out. They had no idea anyone was living in them.

It took time for Muraroot to explain this to his father. It was obvious it was going to take time for information to be interpreted, being passed back and forth for everyone.

Muraroot's father began to explain their occupancy of the structures. Muraroot would then tell it in English. "When our tribe reached this area, many long ages ago, these dwellings were already here. My father says it was even before his grandfather was born. Even then, they appeared to have been vacant for an extremely long time. Whoever had lived here had left pottery, tools and other items we have been using since the beginning. We have no idea who built the structures. No one has ever come back to claim them."

Ricardo turned to David. "Wow. That means the structures could be centuries old, built by some lost civilization." He turned to Muraroot. "How many people are in the tribe?"

"There are about three hundred."

David was surprised. "Three hundred? But I've seen no one except for your friends and now, your father and his friends."

Muraroot chuckled. "Everyone not out hunting, catching fish or doing things are in the houses."

"But everyone is so quiet." David shook his head.

"It is because no one has ever seen outsiders before and they are probably afraid." Muraroot smiled. "We have not seen anyone coming to this area."

David couldn't contain himself any longer. "Okay. I want to know your story. How did you get here? There has to be some logical explanation."

"I can only tell you this. All I can remember is waking up here with my father looking over me. He spoke in a language different from the one we now speak. I do not know how I got here or anything from before. I can only tell you what my father has said."

David was surprised. "How long ago was this?"

"Many, many ages ago. My father said there was a great storm and a big bird was flying high above. He and many others saw and heard it. It was caught in the storm. As they watched, the bird broke into many pieces and they came falling down. He told me I came from the big bird and fell into the trees. That is why they call me Muraroot. It means 'from the sky'. Not very often a big, noisy bird will come flying over and we all hide. Like yesterday. A big, noisy, strange bird came flying in and hovered in front of the cliff. We saw and heard it coming and everyone hid."

David was shocked. "Wait! Wait! Wait! You came from a big bird in the sky? A big bird that came apart?"

"That is what my father has told me. He took care of me and brought me back to good health. Over the time, he helped me learn their language. He took me as his own. That is why I call him my father."

Ricardo interrupted. "You say a big bird came by here yesterday and hovered in front of the cliff?"

Muraroot shook his head in the affirmative. "Yes."

Ricardo bent his head down and spoke quietly. "That had to have been us in the helicopter." He looked at David with distress on his face. "You do realize what he is telling us? He is a survivor of a plane crash. And since there seem to be no others like him here, he must have been the only survivor."

Muraroot looked at Ricardo and David. "That was you? In the noisy bird?"

Ricardo turned to Muraroot. "It was not a bird. It was a helicopter. It is a machine that carries people into the air. From what you have just told us, you were in another kind of flying machine when you came here. It was not a bird."

"But my father described it. It had wings like a bird."

David couldn't believe his ears. "Ricardo. You're right. He was in a plane. A plane has crashed somewhere around here. We need to look into this." He turned to Muraroot. "Do you know where your father found you?"

"He has never taken me there but I am sure he knows where it is." He turned to his father and spoke. Finishing with his father, he spoke in English again. "Yes. My father says he knows exactly where the place is but it is not close. It is up by the lake."

"Would he mind taking us to see the area?" David was anxious.

"My father said he can do that but we need to wait until tomorrow. It is too late to go now. It is almost time to eat. My father wants you both to join us to eat. Then, we will talk more before going to bed."

Ricardo looked at David. "I will go back to the other side and contact Miguel and let him know what is happening. Is there anything you want me to tell him?"

"Tell him to fly back to Barcelos, refuel and get more supplies. Tell him to take his time. No rush. Something tells me we might be here for a while. When he returns, he can call us on the walkie-talkie. I'll ask Muraroot if it's possible to clear a large enough area in front of the cliff for Miguel to land closer. Oh. Tell him to bring back at least a hundred rolls of toilet paper and about the same number of bars of soap. I have a feeling such things don't exist here."

Ricardo got up to go contact Miguel. "Will do. Landing out front? That could take some doing to find a place. But it would not hurt to try." He turned to Muraroot. "I am going to contact our friend on the mountain in the helicopter to let him know everything is all right."

Muraroot smiled. "One of my father's friends can go with you."

Ricardo shook his head. "That would be terrific."

Muraroot spoke to one of the men. The man and Ricardo left the house.

David looked at Muraroot and smiled. "This is so amazing. I can't believe it's happening. Many years ago, I was told it would."

A questioning look came to Muraroot's face. "You knew this was going to happen? I do not understand."

David nodded. "Yes. I knew this was going to happen. But I didn't realize it was going to happen here. I thought it was going to happen in the western part of the United States."

Muraroot still didn't understand. "The United States?"

"Yes. I'll explain later. What I want to know is what do you remember?"

"I cannot remember anything before I woke up here many ages ago. I remember nothing from before that time and I only know I got here the way my father told me. I have no idea how I know and understand the language you and I speak. I just do."

"Well, it's very clear to me you have some connection with an English-speaking country. And I'll bet it's the United States. The only way we're going to be able to find out where you came from is to do some research into plane crashes, occurring many years ago. It's going to take some time."

"When your friend, Ricardo, gets back, we will go to the pool and wash up before we eat." Muraroot gave a big smile.

David shook his head. "I sure wish I knew how long ago it was you got here. It would make it so much easier doing the research."

Muraroot bent his head down. "I am so sorry I cannot help you. All I can tell you is it was a long time ago."

David smiled. "Not to worry. It's not important right now. But you have to have a history before you got here. Haven't you ever wondered about that?"

Muraroot shook his head. "It never really seemed important. I was here and I thought that is all there was."

"Well, trust me. I'm going to do some research into this. I have a feeling there are people wondering about you. Before you came here, there had to have been people who cared about you and loved you. They deserve to know you're still here. I'll bet they all think you're dead."

Muraroot tilted his head. "You know. I never thought about that. The people here care for me and love me and I never thought beyond that."

Just then, Ricardo returned. "Miguel told me it might take a day or two to get everything together and come back up here. I told him to take his time and not to worry." He added. "He was very glad there was nothing hostile here."

David clapped his hand on the table. "Excellent! That'll give us some time to try and clear a place down below the cliff."

Muraroot stood up and smiled. "Now that Ricardo is here, let us go to the pool and wash up before we eat."

Ricardo clapped his hands. "Sounds good. Lead the way."

David and Ricardo followed Muraroot. He led them on several paths between some of the structures and finally down a long set of narrow steps to the floor of the inner valley. The path he took eventually led them to a large pool of water.

David stopped in his tracks with a shocked look on his face. "Oh, my God! I don't believe it!" He turned to Ricardo. "Remember what I told you what Lorie said? About the carved stone snake near water? I don't believe it!"

At the head of the pool against a cliff, there was a small waterfall, pouring into the pool, constantly supplying fresh water to the pool. Next to the waterfall was a huge stone carving of the head of a snake. The carved body came down and formed a wall completely around the pool. At the lower end, there was a spillway, leading into a small creek.

Ricardo looked at the carving. "Damn! Your Lorie sure was right on the mark. This is incredible. I sure would not mind having a talk with her one day."

Muraroot pointed at the snake carving. "We have always believed the snake was there to keep evil spirits out of the water. It is always clean and refreshing. Come. Let us get washed." He began removing the little clothes he was wearing. Soon, he jumped into the pool.

David shook his head. He began to giggle as he took off his clothes.

Ricardo began removing his clothes and turned to David. "What is so funny?"

David continued to snicker. "I almost expected him to say. 'Come on in! The water's fine!'"

Ricardo grinned. "Okay. I get it now." He paused. "With what you told me, regarding Lorie's predictions, the other guy in New England, whose reading had a carved snake in it, just has to be Muraroot. His name starts with 'M' and there is the snake." He began to laugh. "David. Meet your future partner."

They both roared with laughter and climbed into the pool.

Muraroot splashed around in the water, rubbing his body with his hands and scratching them through his hair and beard. "What is funny?"

Ricardo called out. "David will explain it to you soon enough."

David called out. "My kingdom! My kingdom! For a bar of soap!"

Ricardo understood. "I see why you wanted Miguel to bring some. I do not even want to know what they use for toilet paper."

After a while, they all climbed out of the pool. Since there were no towels to dry themselves, they just got dressed. Muraroot led them back up to his father's house. Ricardo and David were surprised to see there was food already on the table. They all sat down. His father had already begun to eat.

David noticed there were no utensils, only pointed sticks for them to use to eat with. He turned to Ricardo with a big grin on his face. "I must admit it does look interesting but I don't want to know what any of it is. I can only imagine."

Ricardo snickered. "If you really want to know, I can ask."

David shook his head. "Never mind. That's okay."

They all ate quietly. There was no conversation.

By the time they finished eating, the sun was well below setting and it was getting dark. Muraroot led them to a room in one of the structures where there were two piles of palm leaves covered with animal skins. "You and Ricardo can sleep here. My room is down this way." He pointed in a direction. "My father has said he will lead you tomorrow to where they found me a long time ago." He smiled and left the room.

David looked around the room. "Well. It's definitely not the Ritz. What can I say?"

Ricardo began to laugh. "Hey! At least it is not the stone floor."

They both began to laugh even harder.

CHAPTER IX

The next morning, under the direction of Muraroot, a group of men went down in front of the cliff and began removing the growth and vegetation in order for the helicopter to land when Miguel returned. David noticed they were using stone axes to do the job.

Ricardo was pleased and surprised at how quickly they removed undergrowth and small trees from a fairly large flat area. "It is looking very good. I think the area is large enough for Miguel to land. What do you think?" He looked in David's direction.

"Looks good to me. All we have to do now is wait till he gets here. I swear. With what I had to do this morning out behind those trees, I can't wait for the toilet paper to arrive."

Ricardo grinned. "I know what you mean."

Muraroot spoke up. "I see my father and his men are coming down the ladder. It is time to head out."

Shortly, the group headed in a north-easterly direction. Eventually, they reached the narrow river, running from north to south in the middle of the valley. David noticed there were several dugout canoes pulled up on the bank. It was obvious they were used to go fishing and to get to the far side of the river. He also wondered how many piranha were in the water and started to giggle nervously.

Muraroot called out. "What is funny?"

David shook his head. "I was just wondering if there were any dangerous fish in these waters."

Ricardo yelled out. "I got it! I got it! Piranha! Yeah! We should be very careful."

Muraroot responded. "There are many things in the water. You must be careful."

Muraroot and his father led everyone to two of the canoes. "Six will get in one and six will get in the other." He looked at David and Ricardo. "We and three others will get in the second canoe. My father and his men will get in the first. They will lead us. They know where they are going."

The first canoe pulled away with four of the men rowing. The second soon followed with Muraroot and three others rowing. David was rather surprised. Even with the current in the water flowing south, they were moving at a pretty good clip upstream.

After some time, David began to chuckle.

Ricardo called out. "Now, what is funny?"

David continued to chuckle. "I sure am glad I didn't have to row. I'd have been exhausted twenty minutes ago."

Ricardo and Muraroot began to laugh.

Muraroot smiled. "David. If ever you need someone to row for you, let me know. I will do it for you."

Ricardo smiled and flexed his eyebrows. "Yep. I am pretty sure. He is the one." He and David chuckled as David shook his head.

David estimated it was just over an hour of rowing upstream when they arrived at a fairly large lake. Slowly, the lead canoe began to head toward the eastern bank. The second canoe followed. Hitting the bank, everyone was soon out of the canoes. Several of the men pulled them farther up onto the bank.

This done, Muraroot's father began to lead the group in a north-easterly direction along the edge of the lake. Almost immediately, the party headed into the eastern jungle. Several of the men had their axes to remove undergrowth in the way. After about ten minutes, Muraroot's father stopped and spoke to him.

Muraroot turned to Ricardo and David. "My father said we are almost there. We will have to look through much undergrowth to find it."

They continued forward and almost instantly came upon a large piece of wing, containing two engines. The propellers were severely bent and damaged.

David was shocked. "Oh, my God! This wing piece! From what I can tell, there must have been four engines. We're talking about a pretty good-sized passenger plane. Wow! Most airlines stopped using prop-driven planes ages ago." He quickly took several pictures.

Muraroot's father called out to him and spoke.

Muraroot turned to David and Ricardo. "My father said he is now going to take us to where he found me." A concerned look came to his face.

David saw this. "Muraroot. What's the matter?"

"I feel strange. I have never been here before."

David walked over and grabbed his upper arm, looking him directly in the face. "Everything will be all right. Not to worry. We are here for you."

Muraroot smiled. "I am not sure why but I am glad you are here with me. I feel it will make it easier for me to accept."

Everyone headed deeper into the jungle.

They walked for about ten minutes when they came across another piece of what looked to be a section of the side of the plane. No glass remained in the windows. Again, David took more pictures.

Ricardo commented. "If the plane had not been made of aluminum, there would be no sign of it ever being here. It would have rusted away in the weather after all the years."

They continued onward.

David was sure the undergrowth and vines were probably hiding many more pieces of the plane. He now began to wonder how many people were on it when disaster struck.

After some twenty more minutes, they saw Muraroot's father stop and look all around. It seemed he was looking for some landmark to pinpoint where he was. Suddenly, he let out a loud 'Ah' sound and pointed in a direction left of where they were. He led everyone in that direction. Eventually, he stopped and pointed.

There on the ground almost totally covered with vines was what looked like the remains of a set of seats. He turned to Muraroot and spoke.

Muraroot looked at David and Ricardo. "My father tells me he found me there in the seat on the right. I was strapped in and not awake. He said it looked like the seats had fallen through the canopy of the trees, breaking its fall. At the time, he and others looked around and found no one else alive."

Several 'clicking' sounds came from David's camera. He lowered the camera, looking down at the decaying seat. "Muraroot. Does any of this bring back any memories to you?"

He looked at David. "I am sorry. But it does not. I remember nothing of this. The first thing I remember is waking up in my father's house. Nothing before."

David looked around the area. "Ask your father if he knows of any piece that has a name or numbers on it."

Muraroot turned to his father, speaking and gesturing. His father smiled and let out another 'Ah' sound. He started leading them in a northerly direction.

As they walked along, they passed two more sections of the side of the plane and a wheel mount before reaching their destination. Again, David took more photographs.

Finally, Muraroot's father pointed. There, among the vines and undergrowth, was the crumpled tail section of the plane. Time had taken its toll on the paint, showing the logo and number. But they were still visible.

David was shocked but ecstatic. "Oh, my God! It was a Constellation! They carried a good number of people. Wow! This had to have happened years ago as the Constellation went out of service when jet planes took to the skies. I'll bet this crash happened in the nineteen sixties." He stared at the ruins of the triple tail covered with vines. "This truly is a major piece of the puzzle. With this information, we should be able to discover the whole story of this flight." He took more photographs then turned to Muraroot. "And we'll finally be able to discover where you came from and your history." A big smile filled his face.

Muraroot looked at the tail of the plane and then at David. A big smile filled his face as well. "I am glad you are here with me."

Ricardo looked hard at the numbers and the logo. "Okay. There is something very familiar about that logo. But I cannot quite put my finger on it."

David turned to Muraroot. "Tell your father we thank him very much for bringing us here. What we've discovered will help tremendously. We can now return to your father's house."

Muraroot turned to his father and told him what David said. They started back to the river.

It was very late afternoon when they arrived back, climbing up to the dwellings. Ricardo got on the walkie-talkie just to see if Miguel had returned. There was no response, so they all returned to Muraroot's father's house.

Muraroot turned to David and Ricardo. "Before we eat, let us go get washed." They headed down to the pool.

David was pleasantly surprised at how refreshing it was to get into the water. It seemed to remove much of the tension of the day.

After eating, the light of day was waning and everyone was ready to head to sleep. All went to their rooms to retire.

As David lay on his bedding, he was very pleased with the accomplishment of the day. He could only imagine where it would lead.

The next day, there was no sign of Miguel, so Muraroot, his father, David and Ricardo sat talking all day. There was interest in the history of the tribe but there really wasn't much to tell. Before they'd come to the dwellings, the tribe had been rather nomadic in nature. The dwellings gave them a place of permanence to do their hunting, fishing and gathering.

Muraroot's father wanted to know of the outside world. It took time for Muraroot to do the translating but his father seemed to like all he heard. He did understand there were problems facing people but he was extremely interested in things such as healthcare, education and discovering new things. He wondered if there was a possibility their tribe could somehow meld into the society of the outside world. This really surprised David and Ricardo.

Muraroot agreed. "It would be wonderful for people to be able to get educated and learn new things. It would also be a very good thing if anyone got sick or hurt there was a place for them to go and be healed." He paused for a moment. "What if a tribal community was established somewhere near a civilized and commercial area? It would keep members of the tribe within the group but also allow them to have access to the outside world and even possibly find work."

Ricardo and David were astonished. How amazing they'd accept such a concept.

David turned to Muraroot. "You do realize it would be an extreme change for the tribe. Let us just say a community was constructed for the tribe just upriver from where the Rio Demini runs into the Rio Negro. It would keep the tribe segregated yet close enough to Barcelos to allow people to go into town, explore and get to know what civilization is all about. What can I say?"

Muraroot explained this to his father who became incredibly excited about the idea. With further discussion, they realized if they worked with the Brazilian government, it might actually be possible for it to happen. Obviously, it would take time but it just might be able to become a reality.

"Muraroot. If we could get permission from the Brazilian government for a large parcel of land, I could easily contribute around a hundred thousand dollars toward the construction of a community near the Rio Demini. Hey! It could be the beginning. And since you know the language and can speak English, you could teach others. With education, some of the tribe and especially the younger children would be able to learn two languages or more. You, Ricardo and I could go speak to proper authorities and get the ball rolling. I'll bet there might even be some way for the tribe to be subsidized by the government until people could get on their own and make their own way. Then, everyone would be taken care of, regardless."

Ricardo was surprised. "You would actually donate a hundred thousand American dollars for such a thing?"

David smiled. "Why not? It's only money. I've been very fortunate in my life and I believe when people have been as lucky as me, they should share the bounty. Because of my best friend in Atlanta, I make more than four times that every year due to his proper and smart investing."

Ricardo's mouth fell open. "REALLY!? I definitely would not mind talking to your friend in Atlanta. Do you think it would be possible?"

David looked right at Ricardo. "I told you. You have to come for a visit sometime and meet everyone. I wasn't joking when I told you that." He paused as a big smile came to his face and he shook his head. He tilted his head as something came to his mind.

Ricardo had a questioning look on his face. "What? What is it? I can tell you are thinking about something."

David shook his head and smiled. "I just had a thought. If you come to Atlanta, there's a friend I know there who you should meet. He's done very well financially as he has done investing with my friend, James. He's smart as a whip. Definitely not a dummy. He's a rather attractive guy. Short like me. But totally outrageous and can be really outspoken at times. He's got a terrific personality. A lot of fun. Never was good at relationships. He never picked the right guys. He needs someone strong. Someone who can stand up to him. He really needs a MAN. And, Ricardo. Strangely enough. You're just the kind of MAN he's looking for and just doesn't know it. I have no idea what you like about a person, physically or mentally."

Ricardo flexed his eyebrows and smiled. "Believe it or not, I really like short guys and one with a bit of spice can make a relationship fun and lasting."

David continued. "Well. He'd definitely be a handful. Funny. I believe if anyone could tame him, you could be the one. I also believe you could be just the one to give him love. If you hold him close and show him love, I don't think either of you would regret it. Something tells me he has a lot of love to give to the right man."

"What is his name?"

David looked right at Ricardo. "Michael. His name is Michael."

With a smile on his face, Ricardo thrust his right arm straight up into the air, his hand in a fist and he cried out. "Excellent!" He yelled out. "Michael! Yes!"

Periodically during the day, Ricardo would go to the east front of the complex and use the walkie-talkie to see if Miguel had returned yet. There was no sign of him. Finally, he returned from his last attempt of the day. He looked at David with a big grin on his face. "I guess he is having a real problem finding those hundred bars of soap and hundred rolls of toilet paper."

David just smiled, closed his eyes and shook his head.

Late the next morning, Ricardo went out front again to see if Miguel had arrived. He had and was up on the mountain. Ricardo instructed him to fly down and land in front of the complex.

Everyone went out front to watch the helicopter land. Very shortly, it was visible overhead and slowly descending to the cleared area in front.

Muraroot turned to David and Ricardo. "So, that is what you call a helicopter, not a bird." His face was filled with excitement.

Ricardo slapped Muraroot on the back. "You are absolutely correct."

Ricardo continued. "Actually, some people do call them 'Whirlybirds' but let's not confuse the issue."

David looked at Ricardo. "Thank you."

Several of the tribesmen lowered several rope ladders, anticipating the supplies. Muraroot, David and Ricardo climbed down, along with several of the other men to help unload the helicopter.

Many looked down at the helicopter from above. They were terrified of it.

Miguel shut off the engines and slowly, the propellers began to slow and finally stopped spinning.

"Miguel! How are you? Thank you so very much for getting things for us." David waved at Miguel.

Miguel climbed down off the helicopter and walked toward David. "Are you ready for this? I think I bought every bar of soap and every roll of toilet paper in Barcelos. I hope you do not mind but I brought nearly two hundred rolls of toilet paper."

David was overjoyed. "I think that was probably a very good idea. And just wait till you hear the idea everyone has come up with. It'll be truly revolutionary for the tribe. Let me introduce you to Muraroot and his father. Muraroot's father is the tribe's leader."

All shook hands but no one spoke. Just smiled.

Miguel looked at Muraroot and then at his father. A questioning look came to his face. "Ah. Something is wrong with this picture. This is Muraroot? And his father? Is someone pulling my leg?"

Ricardo answered. "It is a very strange story. It will make sense when you hear it."

Miguel continued to look back and forth at Muraroot and his father. "I bet it will."

The propellers having stopped, the men crept closer to the helicopter. Miguel noticed they were afraid and walked over, opening the side door. He climbed in, lifted up a box and held it out to one of the men. Finally, one step forward and took the box.

Miguel called out to David. "I have a feeling no one wants to come in here to get the supplies. I guess I will have to hand them out."

Muraroot turned to the men and spoke to them in the language of the tribe. Then, he walked over to the helicopter and climbed in. After a moment, two of the men got closer, stopped, looked in the doorway and made a loud 'Ah' sound. One climbed in, turned to the others and spoke to them. That's all it took. They weren't afraid anymore and started unloading the supplies.

Miguel turned to Muraroot. "Thank you. Thank you very much." He gave a big smile.

Muraroot smiled. "I am glad I could help." He turned to the men and spoke to them then turned to Miguel. "I was telling them where they could store the supplies."

Miguel stopped cold. "Oh, my God! He speaks English? You have to be kidding. Now, I know there IS a totally weird story here."

David and Ricardo called out in unison. "Yep!"

David looked at Miguel. "Miguel! Throw out my satchel. Ricardo's, too. There are some things in mine I need like more rolls of film."

He did as asked. Grabbing his own satchel, he climbed down.

Muraroot also climbed down and suggested they all go to his father's house, so they could talk.

All, finally getting seated at the table, the conversation continued. David explained the idea of the entire tribe moving down near Barcelos.

Miguel was surprised. "Wow. That really would be a huge change in what they are used to. But it will help them with having access to healthcare, supplies and a greater comfort of living. Did you also tell them about the problems that exist in the world? Like crime?"

Muraroot spoke. "Yes. He did. But my father discussed it with our people and all agree the advantages outweigh the bad."

Miguel commented. "I have a feeling the Brazilian government would want to get involved as well as people who study native cultures. Muraroot would have a big hand in helping them understand the language. And speaking of Muraroot and his ability to speak English and obviously NOT looking like his father. Okay. What IS his story?"

David agreed. "Yes. We were struck by the same questions. But we found out he came here in a plane."

Miguel interrupted. "IN A PLANE???!! WHAT!!!?"

David held up his hand. "Let me finish. It was in a plane... crash. Up north of here." He reached for his satchel and pulled out his notebook and pen. "We were up there and saw some of the wreckage. There were no other survivors. But on the tail section was a logo that looked like this. I also took a few pictures of the logo and number on the tail." He drew a likeness of the logo on the blank page then turned it toward Miguel.

Miguel looked at it and his face scrunched up into a questioning expression. After a few seconds, he called out. "Wait! That does look familiar. It is very similar to the logo of one of the airlines here. Rio Express Airways. But I know of no crashes. This must have happened a very long time ago. We will have to look into it when we get back to Barcelos." He paused a moment. "We may even have to go to Rio de Janeiro to check it out."

David was pleased. "Miguel. You may have got the ball rolling on this sooner than we thought. We're going to do what is necessary to find out. Muraroot deserves to know where he came from."

Miguel questioned again. "You mean he doesn't know?"

Muraroot looked at Miguel. "I have no memory of anything in my whole life before waking up with my father looking over me here. I did not even know it was a plane crash until I actually got to see the location just yesterday."

Miguel shook his head. "Wow. This really is something. No recollection at all. No wonder you are still here. You knew nothing else. Wow. David is right. You deserve to know your history." He looked at Muraroot. "I promise you. We will do our best and find out your history as soon as possible."

CHAPTER X

Over the next two days, David and Ricardo helped everyone understand how to use toilet paper and the soap. Both were a welcome to the community. In the meantime, Miguel flew back to Barcelos to bring back as many toothbrushes and paste as possible.

Muraroot's father was so happy for him. He knew that Muraroot was going to go back with David, Ricardo and Miguel and was eventually and finally going to find out where he came from.

Muraroot explained he wouldn't be leaving forever but would always be in touch. He would also be involved in the transition to their new location when and if all was approved by the government.

A few days later, David, Ricardo, Miguel and Muraroot flew back early to Barcelos. First, on the agenda, was to get Muraroot some clothes. Wearing only his native attire, he definitely turned heads when they arrived and headed to the shops and hotel.

The hotel desk clerk was quite surprised when he saw Muraroot and could not stop looking at how he was dressed in his native attire.

David looked at the clerk. "It's a very long story. He's been lost in the wilderness a very long time. We found him and have brought him back to help him find out who he really is."

The desk clerk smiled. "I am sure it must be a very interesting story. Let me see about getting him set up with a room."

Muraroot looked at David and interrupted. "Is it possible I can stay in the same room as you?"

The clerk responded. "There are two double beds in the room. I see no problem."

Muraroot smiled. "Very good."

David turned to everyone. "Okay, folks. Let's get to our rooms and get ready for something to eat. How about we all meet down at the restaurant in about forty-five minutes? That'll give Muraroot time to clean up and get into some of his new clothes, too."

All agreed and they headed to their rooms.

David and Muraroot went to their room. David showed him how the shower worked and the towels. He laid out the set of new clothes, socks and sneakers.

Muraroot called out from the shower. "I really like this warm water. It is very nice. I really like the soap, too. It makes my skin feel so clean."

After his shower, David showed him how to use the toothbrush and paste. "The Listerine is for gargling after you brush your teeth, not drinking." He took a swig and showed Muraroot about gargling, swishing it through the teeth then spitting it out. "And this is a deodorant stick." He showed how to use it.

Next, David got out the pair of scissors, electric hair clippers and razor from his own toiletries, so he could trim Muraroot's beard, stache and hair. He had him sit on a chair in the bathroom and wrapped a big towel around his neck, so he could do the trimming. "I use the hair clippers with an attachment to trim my beard when it gets too long. It'll help me cut some of your hair." When finished, he helped him dress and put on his new sneakers.

Finally, the finished and refurbished Muraroot stood up. David couldn't believe how really handsome he was. "I swear. When you get back into society, you're going to have women fawning all over you. Trust me. You're going to have to beat them off with a stick." He didn't want to say anything, regarding what Lorie had said since there was no indication of Muraroot's orientation. She could have been wrong. But he did sense they would at least be good friends.

Muraroot just smiled.

They opened the door and went down to eat. When they entered the dining room, all were astonished at the transformation in Muraroot.

After everyone ate, they all went out and sat on the outdoor patio for a while. Eventually, all returned to their rooms to get some rest. The previous days had been quite exhausting.

David went in and took a shower. He came out of the bathroom, drying himself with a towel. He looked at Muraroot. "I give you the choice of beds. Pick one." Muraroot picked the one closest to the windows, pulled back the sheets and got in it.

David set the towel on the nearby chair and got in his bed. "Muraroot. Goodnight, my friend. Sleep well. This should be a big difference from the palm leaves you're used to."

Muraroot clapped his hands. "Yes. It is very comfortable. Very nice. I like it."

David lay there, recalling all that had happened over the last days. He could only imagine what would be taking place in the next days to come.

Just then, Muraroot spoke quietly. "David. Thank you so much for what you are doing for me and my tribe. Your kindness is so amazing."

"You're very welcome. You deserve to know your history and where you come from. Even your tribal father knows and realizes this. He would never have sent you along if he didn't believe it was important."

"I just wanted you to know, I am very thankful. Goodnight and see you in the morning."

There was quiet and soon they were both asleep.

James looked out at all his guests. "Yes. Neither realized it but that night was the beginning of David and Muraroot becoming closer together. This was the beginning of a relationship that would grow and endure. Both were beginning to sense the feelings, building in each of them for the other."

He immediately looked over to Michael. "And no suggestive remarks from you?"

Michael cried out. "What? ME!?"

The room erupted in laughter.

James continued. "David arranged to have several helicopter airdrops of supplies to the tribe. Also, in the meantime, David contacted a private plane to take them to Rio de Janeiro to look into the airline. Miguel left his helicopter in Barcelos. Yes. It took time but finally, after some exhaustive digging into old files, an answer came."

"The logo belonged to the predecessor of a present airline. It was a flight coming from Bogotá in July of nineteen sixty-one and never arrived in Rio."

David, Ricardo and Miguel cried out in unison. "NINETEEN SIXTY-ONE???!!"

Miguel shook his head. "Damn! That was twenty-four years ago."

A large map was pulled out and the representative of the airline explained the route the plane normally took.

Ricardo was surprised. "Oh, my God. Here is where the wreckage is located." He pointed at the map.

The representative shook his head. "That is way off course. No wonder it was never found. I have a feeling no one was looking so far off the normal flight path." He paused and looked at Muraroot. "And this gentleman is the only one who survived?"

Everyone shook their heads in the affirmative.

Muraroot asked. "Is there any information about the flight? I mean. I wonder why I would have been on it?"

The airline representative shook his head. "I am so sorry. There is nothing else in this file about it. We are going to have to look more into this. There must be some information on this somewhere. Probably in our archives and old newspaper accounts. Especially, since it was lost. Even after this length of time, the relatives of those on board deserve to have closure."

David saw Muraroot looked disappointed. "Not to worry. This is just the beginning. We're going to get to the bottom of this. Trust me."

Muraroot smiled at David and winked his right eye. "Thank you. I know you will."

David sighed. "Okay. I don't know about any of you but I need a drink."

Everyone shook their heads in agreement.

Ricardo and Miguel were familiar with Rio and they went to a nice restaurant. After being seated, drinks were ordered all around. Muraroot was still getting used to his gin and tonics.

David was excited. "I've got to explain. Ricardo already knows some of what I'm about to tell you." He looked at Miguel. "And you must promise not to laugh." He was silent for a few moments. "Muraroot and I have a connection, going back a very long way. I've realized this because of his name starting with an 'M' and the stone snake at the pool up in the ruins. I was told about those things twenty-two years ago. At a high school graduation party. By a woman named Lorie. She was a psychic reader." He looked at Miguel and was surprised not to see any questioning expression.

Miguel smiled. "Hey. I have always believed in that stuff. So, not to worry. Keep going. I want to hear it all."

David continued. "The party was in May of nineteen sixty-three. Just before my eighteenth birthday in June. Lorie indicated she had done a reading a few years earlier for a guy who was getting ready to graduate from high school. It was a similar party. She'd seen similar things in his reading. I now believe that person was Muraroot. His reading took place in New England in June of nineteen sixty. Now, I understand why he speaks English. I'm just not sure why he has no memory of his past." He turned to Muraroot. "If you were eighteen by June of nineteen sixty, it means you're forty-three. Three years older than me. And you're from New England." He didn't divulge the information, regarding past lives together. He felt it would be too much information for Muraroot to hear at that time.

Muraroot had a questioning expression on his face. "What is New England?"

Ricardo reached over and patted him on the shoulder. "Not to worry, big guy. You are going to find out if David has anything to do with it." He looked at David. "I know this is going to sound really off-the-wall." He bent his head down and started shaking it.

"What?" David was curious.

Ricardo continued. "What would you think about taking Muraroot to a psychiatrist who is a hypnotist? He just might be able to put him under and do a past regression on him."

"Ricardo! Brilliant! That's a fantastic idea! It just might work. I hope he's capable of being hypnotized. I've heard some people can't be hypnotized."

Ricardo grinned. "Yeah. But the percentages of those are very few."

"My doctor in Atlanta would know of a good one."

Ricardo looked directly at David. "Muraroot cannot leave Brazil. He has no papers or passport. And do you know what he is going to have to do to get one?"

"Well. With his situation, they might make an exception and do a rush job." David smiled. "And I'm sure a few well-placed 'donations' wouldn't hurt."

Ricardo and Miguel both grinned and gave a 'thumbs-up'.

"And while we're waiting for that to happen, I can ask my doctor if he'll talk to one and see if he'd consider coming down here to conduct his services. All expenses paid. Of course, his fee as well. I'll call him immediately."

James smiled. "David called his doctor the next day who referred him to a Doctor Kenneth Johnson. This man is one of Atlanta's leading psychiatrists. David was quite surprised when Doctor Johnson indicated there would be no problem with him coming down in about a week if that was satisfactory. It would be early November. David couldn't complain about that at all."

Being familiar with Rio, Ricardo and Miguel had them located in a very nice hotel close to the beach. David made arrangements for Dr. Johnson to have a room when he got there. The hotel indicated there would be no problem for him to stay as long as he wanted. They had the rooms.

They were in the hotel restaurant when David turned to Miguel and Ricardo. "I hope you guys realize you're still on the payroll. Miguel. We may not be using your helicopter right now but we need your input and moral support."

Both couldn't have been happier, clapping their hands and doing high-fives.

Ricardo took a sip of his cocktail. "I have a confession to make."

Everyone looked at Ricardo.

"David. I have done something that might not sit well with you. I invited a friend of mine over this afternoon. He should be here any minute. He. Ah. He is a reporter for one of Rio's TV stations. I called him when we first got to Rio. When he heard Muraroot's story, he just had to come and meet all of us and do an interview. I hope you are not mad or angry."

"Angry!? Hell No! Another stroke of brilliance! It is obvious! Your mother did NOT raise a stupid child. Just think of the exposure Muraroot will get and the publicity. This could help significantly in getting closer to finding out who he is. Ricardo! Thank you!" David jumped up from the table and started doing the Snoopy Happy Dance.

Muraroot started laughing. "What are you doing?"

David stopped and looked at Muraroot. "It's from a TV cartoon show. A dog called Snoopy and that is the dance he'd do when he was happy."

Muraroot clapped his hands together. "I know a dance!"

Ricardo looked at Muraroot. "Really? Is it one from the tribe?"

"No. I do not know where it comes from. I just know it."

Miguel couldn't resist. "Okay. I want to see it." He looked at everyone. "This should be good."

Muraroot stood up near David who was still standing. He looked at everyone with a smile. "Are you ready?"

Everyone shook their heads in the affirmative, calling out. "Yeah!"

Muraroot took a stance and then started singing out as he moved. "Come on, Baby. Let's do the Twist."

David screamed out. "Holy SHIT!" He instantly joined in with Muraroot.

They both sang and danced together, gyrating across the floor. "Come on, Baby! Let's do the Twist! Take me by my little hand. And go like this. Yee... Aaah Twist. Yeah, baby. Twist. Oooo... Yeah. Just like this. Come on little Miss. And do the Twist." At that, they both stopped, bent over laughing. Ricardo and Miguel were laughing loudly with them. Others in the restaurant couldn't imagine what was going on but all were cheering and clapping at what they saw and heard.

David and Muraroot were still laughing. David turned to everyone in the restaurant and started bowing several times. Muraroot saw what David was doing and followed suit.

Muraroot looked at David and cried out. "You know it! You know it!!! How is it you know my dance!!? And the words, too?" He continued to laugh.

David cried out. "NINETEEN SIXTY! Chubby Checker! Who could EVER forget that dance?" He looked at Muraroot. "It's from your past. Just like your English. You remember that song and the dance. Yep! We're going to find out who you are, where you come from and your history. Don't you worry. It will all come together soon enough."

Not long afterward, someone from the front desk came out, indicating there was a guest wanting to talk to Ricardo. He was from the TV station. Ricardo immediately followed the desk clerk back to the lobby. Shortly, he and another gentleman returned to the restaurant.

"This is my friend, Marco. He is the one I told you about."

Everyone stood and shook hands.

David smiled. "Marco. Please, have a seat."

Marco smiled. "I hope you do not mind but I did bring my camera crew to film while I did the interviews. The story Ricardo told me is so amazing, I wanted there to be some film footage with my news report tonight."

"Marco! Go get them! Tell them to come in. We can take all of this out on the patio." David directed.

In a short period of time, all were assembled out on the patio. Marco directed everyone, so he could conduct the interviews he wanted. "Do not worry if you make any mistakes or fumbles during the interviews. All that can be edited later."

It took almost two hours for all the interviews to be completed. Marco was especially surprised by the information and interview with Muraroot. He did tell everyone he didn't want any information, regarding the location of the tribe or the ancient ruins for fear the wrong individuals might try to go there and cause problems. He had a feeling many high officials in government would take immediate action to protect the tribe and the ruins after his report.

David went up to the room and got several of the thirty-five millimeter slides he'd taken of the tribe, the ruins and the plane. When they first had arrived in Rio, he'd taken many of his rolls of film in to be developed and had gotten them back just the previous day.

Marco was very pleased and asked if he could use several of

them. He indicated he didn't want to use any that might give away the location. Once he was finished copying them, they would be immediately returned to David.

Marco commented. "After I had talked with Ricardo, I called some of the government officials. They indicated officials in Barcelos had already contacted them on the subject. They are looking forward to meeting and talking with all of you. They want to do this first before they send out any archaeologists or other pertinent individuals. When I get back to the station, I will call several of them and let them know where you are. It is possible they may want to come here to talk with you and to meet Muraroot. I hope you do not mind that I took that step."

"Marco! That was a great idea. We'd have no idea who to contact in the governmental offices. This is terrific. Maybe they'll come out here in the next few days." David was extremely pleased.

CHAPTER XI

James looked around the room. "Is everyone still comfortable? Just wanted to check before I continued." He looked over at Michael. "Michael? You've been rather quiet. Are you bored and falling asleep?"

Michael stood up and cried out. "Mommy! Mommy! James is picking on me! MOMMY!"

Everyone roared with continuous laughter. It took a few moments for everyone to finally calm down and for Michael to sit down.

James was still snickering. "Okay. I was just checking. I see you ARE still alive."

Laughter erupted again for a few seconds.

Michael smiled. "You know. That was very nice of David to say all those nice things about me to Ricardo. I need to tell him how much I appreciated it."

James smiled and nodded. "Michael. Everyone knows you're a totally cool guy and definitely a 'one of a kind'. We all love you just the way you are."

Everyone clapped and cheered while Albert grabbed several glasses and refreshed the drinks before James continued.

"Yes. David was quite surprised when two government officials showed up the next day. They'd seen the news report Marco gave the night before and realized this was something of major importance. They were also quite pleased David wanted to make such a large contribution to the relocation of the tribe. After checking maps of the desired location, it was a done deal. Muraroot would be essential in helping linguists learn the language. Both officials indicated they'd get the ball rolling immediately."

"The very next week, Doctor Johnson arrived. His visit was going to hopefully open wide the door closed in Muraroot's mind for so long."

All four went to meet Dr. Johnson at the airport and bring him back to the hotel.

David smiled as he saw Dr. Johnson, coming in their direction. "Doctor Johnson, I presume. Welcome to Rio."

Dr. Johnson smiled as they all shook hands. "Ken. Please, call me Ken. Doctor Johnson seems so formal here." He looked around to take in the surroundings.

Collecting the luggage, they headed to the car.

Arriving at the hotel, David wanted him to rest and relax on his first day. He could get started on Muraroot when he felt the time was right.

They showed Ken to his room.

"Ken, I do hope it's to your liking." David smiled.

"This room is going to be perfect to use when I start working with Muraroot." He turned to Muraroot. "While we're sitting downstairs on the patio, you and I should talk. It'll allow me to get to know more about you."

Muraroot smiled. "Yes. We can do that."

The rest of the day was spent down on the patio with cocktails, eventually moving to the restaurant for dinner. Ken seemed to be quite pleased while talking with Muraroot. "I truly believed this was going to be a very interesting time. And. Hey. I might even get a book deal out of this." A huge grin filled his face.

Everyone couldn't help but laugh at his humor.

Muraroot turned to Ken. "Will it be possible for my friends to be with me when you are doing your hypnosis? I would like them to be there if that is all right. I definitely want David there."

Ken smiled. "Interesting. In all my working career, I've never had such a request. If you have no problem with them being there, I think it'll be perfectly fine. As long as they are quiet and don't interrupt, they can attend the sessions I have with you."

A questioning look came to Muraroot's face. "I noticed you said 'sessions'. I guess this is not going to be finished in one day."

Ken gave a kindly smile. "Muraroot. With your openness and willingness, I believe this is going to go very smoothly. But yes, I believe it's going to take more than one day. We'll take our time. Eventually, we're going to find out exactly who you are and where you came from."

David was happy and raised his glass in the air. "Hear! Hear!"

All sitting at the table raised their glasses and spoke in unison. "Hear! Hear!"

After breakfast the next day, all gathered in Ken's room. Each had brought a chair from their own rooms, so they could sit down.

Ken instructed Muraroot. "I want you to stack up some pillows on the bed over there, lie down against them and get comfortable. I want you totally relaxed before we get started." He turned to the others. "Gentlemen. I also want you all to get comfortable. Not to worry. Each session won't be too terribly long. Maybe thirty minutes to an hour. The only reason one may last longer would be if we stumble on something that can't be completed in that length of time." He chuckled. "One suggestion. In the beginning, while I'm putting Muraroot under, I want you all to turn away and not watch. I don't want any of you accidentally getting hypnotized." A grin filled his face.

All began to snicker.

Ken smiled. "Okay. I think we're all ready." He paused for a moment. "Muraroot. I want you to get totally relaxed. Try to dismiss everything from your mind. I want you to focus on what is swinging in front of you. Is that understood?"

Muraroot quietly spoke. "Yes. I understand. I am trying to clear my mind."

It took a few minutes but finally, Muraroot was under. Ken turned to the others. "You may look this way now."

"Muraroot. During our sessions, I want you to remember everything, so we may discuss it later on. Do you understand?"

"Yes. I will remember everything."

"Good. Now. You and I have been talking recently. Did you find it pleasant or annoying?"

"I enjoyed our conversations."

"Yes. The information you gave me about your tribe and how you became a part of it was very interesting. I thank you for sharing that information."

"But..." Muraroot paused for a moment.

Ken was curious. "Yes? Is there something else?"

"Yes. There is more I have not told you. It is something very important to me but very personal."

"Muraroot. May I ask what this is about?"

"Yes. It is about... David."

Everyone turned and looked at David.

"Is there something wrong with David?"

"Oh! No! No! David is fine. But I am not sure how to explain it. I feel something inside me. I like David. I like David very much. I like being with him. He has been so helpful and kind to me. I can tell he wants the best for me. I want to tell him but I am afraid. I have no right."

Ken had a questioning look on his face. "Muraroot. What is it? It is all right to tell me. I will understand."

"When I am with David, I feel happiness inside me. When I am not with him, I am not as happy. The only way I can explain it is by what I have seen in my time, living with the tribe."

Ken spoke quietly. "Yes. Muraroot, tell me what you mean."

"I have watched men in the tribe when they are interested in a woman of the tribe. They seem to get all crazy inside and when they talk about the woman, they seem to be very happy with smiles on their faces. I have not fully understood what this was because I have never seen a woman in the tribe that made me feel this way. I have never felt that way toward any woman in the tribe. Actually, I have not felt that way toward ANYONE in the tribe. I sometimes used to wonder if there was something wrong with me. But now. I have met David. I know he is not a woman but he does make me feel happy and crazy inside. I just want to run up and grab him and hold him close. Am I wrong to have such feelings for him? Do you think he would be mad at me for having such feelings?"

Ken smiled. "Muraroot. I have a feeling David would totally understand if you talked about this with him. You might be very surprised. I believe he has similar feelings for you." Ken turned and looked at David who had a big smile on his face. "Yes. I think you should talk with David about this."

"I really like David. I like being with him. I do not want him to go away from me. I do not want to lose the warm feeling I have for him inside me."

"Not to worry. When you and David go to your room tonight, talk to him about this. I don't think you'll be disappointed."

"Thank you very much. That has been a big help to me. I will do it. Tonight. I will tell him of the feelings I have for him inside me. Thank you."

"Muraroot. Is there anything else you'd like to discuss?"

"No. That is the only thing that has been bothering me. I am so glad you told me it was all right to talk about it with David."

"Muraroot. I think that's enough for right now. This is a good beginning. You have taken a very big step today. There's no need to rush things. We'll talk again tomorrow morning. Will that be all right with you?"

"Yes. Tomorrow morning. Very good. I cannot wait to tell David. I am very excited." A huge smile covered Muraroot's face.

"Muraroot. I'm going to count backward from five to one. When I reach one, I want you to wake and be alert. But. I do not want you to remember we have had this conversation except the part for you to discuss the feelings you have for David when you both go to your room tonight. Do you understand?"

"Yes. Yes, I do. But I thought you told me to remember everything, so we can talk about it later."

"You are correct. But in this instance, I do not want you to remember right now. You will understand in time. Do you understand?"

Muraroot smiled. "Yes. I understand."

Ken continued. "Okay. I'm going to start counting now." Ken counted very slowly. "Five..... Four..... Three..... Two..... One."

At that, Muraroot opened his eyes with a big smile on his face. He looked around at everyone. "Did I do all right? Did I say anything important?"

Ken looked at him and smiled. "You did very well. It was an excellent beginning. We'll continue tomorrow morning after breakfast."

Muraroot was very happy. He made a fist with his right hand and thrust his arm straight into the air. "Oh! Yeah!"

The rest of the day was spent on the patio, allowing time for Ken to get acquainted with Miguel and Ricardo. The time was very relaxing.

After dinner, everyone went out onto the patio again for a final cocktail before heading to bed. The day had been very restful for all.

Ricardo stood up. "Well, gentlemen, I think I am going to call it for the evening. What time does everyone want to meet for breakfast?"

David smiled. "How does nine o'clock sound? That way no one will feel rushed."

Everyone was in agreement and shortly thereafter, all headed to their rooms for the night.

Muraroot took his shower followed by David. When he emerged from the bathroom, he saw Muraroot, sitting on the edge of his bed. He went and sat on his bed directly across from Muraroot and looked directly at him. "I have a feeling there's something you want to talk about." He smiled.

"Yes. Yes, there is." Muraroot smiled. "I am not really sure where to begin." He paused and bent his head down. After a moment he picked his head up and looked at David. "I am not sure how to say this without it sounding awkward. But it started when I first saw you. There was something about you. I was drawn to you. It is like there was some connection I had with you. As time went on, I liked being around you. I enjoyed your company. You started becoming important to me. You have been so helpful and kind to me. David. I see how hard you are working to help me find out who I am and where I come from."

He shook his head. "David. I know it is not the way it is with most everyone but I have feelings for you deep inside me. I am so afraid you will go away and I will lose you. If that happened, I am afraid part of me would die. I know it sounds crazy but I cannot help it. If you only knew how many nights I have laid in bed and wanted to come over and get in your bed and hold you and tell you I care about you. I did not do it because I did not want you to think I am crazy."

David looked at Muraroot and smiled. "I am glad you told me. I have had feelings for you as well. Many years ago I was told I would meet you and come to care very much for you. I was told you and I had shared time together in many past lives and we were meant to be together in this one. Muraroot. I've come to care very much for you and I can't imagine being without you. I, too, am beginning to have deep feelings for you."

Muraroot had a frown on his face. "Maybe when we find out who I am, you may think badly of me and your feelings will change.

And that would be all right. I would understand. I might have been a bad person before."

David shook his head. "I doubt that. You're too good now for you to have been a bad person in the past. I think when we find out everything, we're going to find out you're a very fine man. Also, since you have no knowledge of the world out here, you'll be meeting others who you may have feelings for. And that would be all right, too. I don't want you to feel any obligations toward me just because I'm helping you. The way we feel shouldn't have strings attached or obligations attached."

"Okay. I know. But I cannot imagine meeting someone else who makes me feel the same way I feel about you."

David patted Muraroot's leg. "Let's just take our time and go slow. There's an old expression. 'Haste makes waste.' We need to take our time and build what we feel, slowly."

Muraroot smiled. "I agree. We will take our time. We will go slow."

David gave a big smile. "Yes. We will."

Muraroot tilted his head to the side and spoke quietly. "Would it be all right to sleep with you tonight?"

David smiled as he shook his head in the affirmative. "Yes. I would like that."

They both stood and hugged each other tightly.

From that night forward, the love they felt and shared would grow stronger and lasting.

CHAPTER XII

The next day after breakfast, they all gathered in Ken's room again. Everyone sat where they had the previous day. Once settled, it began.

Ken looked around at everyone. "We're going to start just as we did yesterday. I want to make sure everyone is comfortable. Okay. Now, Muraroot. I want you to relax again and clear your mind."

Just as the day before, Muraroot was under in no time.

Ken began. "Are you doing all right?"

Muraroot smiled. "Yes, I am very good. I am so glad you told me to talk with David. It turned out great. Thank you very much."

Ken smiled and looked over at David who had a big smile on his face. He turned back to Muraroot. "That's good. With this session, I want you to remember everything we talk about, so we can discuss it when you're out of the session. Is that clear?"

"Yes. I will remember everything. Will it be all right to talk about how I feel about David?"

Ken smiled. "Yes. I think that will be just fine. I know everyone will be happy for you."

A big smile filled Mararoot's face. He thrust his right fist into the air and yelled out. "Oh Yeah!"

After a moment, Ken continued. "We're going to try and reach back into your life when you were much younger. Do you think you can do that?"

Muraroot smiled. "I will try. Let me know how far back you want to go."

Ken suggested. "I'm going to let you decide. You tell me and we'll begin there. Is that okay with you?"

Muraroot agreed. "Excellent." After a pause, he spoke. "I have a very good friend. He's coming over for a visit. A sleepover."

"How old are you?"

"I'm fourteen. It's summer. Nineteen fifty-six. My friend, Kevin, is the same age. We just got out of the eighth grade. This fall we're going to be high school Freshmen." He started laughing.

Ken asked. "What's so funny?"

He laughed again. "I just realized. I'm using contractions. I'd forgotten about them and how to use them till now. Yeah. Don't. You're. Haven't. I'll." He laughed hard. "Yeah. I'd forgotten till now. Doctor Ken. Can I use them from now on?"

Ken chuckled. "Yes. Of course, you can." He shook his head. "You're fourteen. What is significant about this time, making you pick it to start?"

"It was the first time we played with the Ouija board. Yeah. There was something about doing it that seemed to change my life."

David, Ricardo and Miguel looked at one another but said nothing.

"You had a Ouija board?" Ken continued.

"Yes. Kevin and I had gone shopping and there was a group of people out in the parking lot. They were like gypsies and had a booth."

David's mouth fell open, remembering the time he bought his Ouija board.

"There was a kindly old gypsy lady there and I bought the board from her. She told me how to use it and to make sure I asked for a guide. Kevin and I were very excited." He chuckled slyly.

Ken responded. "What's funny?"

"When I brought it home, I did something to the board. On the back in one of the corners." He giggled. "I put my initials. 'MF'."

David gasped and his eyes bulged.

Everyone turned and looked at David.

David shook his head, raised his hand and spoke quietly. "I'll explain later."

Muraroot continued. "Kevin was coming for a sleepover that night, so we got it out and did what the gypsy lady said to do. We put the board on our knees, sat quietly and put our fingers on the planchette. I then asked if there was anyone out there. Of course, that made us both start to giggle. But, suddenly, the planchette slowly moved to 'YES'. Kevin and I looked at one another and we both swore we hadn't pushed it. That's when I asked who it was. I was sure it was a guide like the gypsy lady had said."

Ken asked. "Did you find out who it was?"

"Yes. That's when the planchette moved and spelled out a name."

Ken questioned. "What was the name?"

"It was Ishmael."

David gasped and had a shocked look on his face. He almost fell out of his chair.

Ken looked at David and saw the expression and what happened. He whispered. "Are you all right?"

David whispered. "Yes. Yes. I'm sorry. I'll explain later."

Ken turned to Muraroot. "Ishmael. Did he become your guide?"

"Yes. It was very interesting. He told us many things we really didn't understand but it was fun. Especially, when we realize neither of us had pushed the planchette."

"Do you remember any of the things he told you?"

"Ishmael said Kevin would move to California in the next year which actually happened. Told him to be very careful of sharks when swimming in the ocean. I never heard from him again. That was kind of sad as he was a really nice friend. I hope he didn't get eaten by sharks. Ishmael also told me I'd meet a lady in a few years. She'd give me information important to know."

"Did Ishmael tell you who she would be?"

"Oh. Yes. Her name would be Lorie."

Again, David's mouth fell open and he shook his head. Information from his own past was becoming clearer and clearer.

Ken continued. "Was there anything else?"

"No." He paused a moment. "Wait. Ishmael told me to remember a name. David. Yes. That's the name. He'd be very important in my life. I'd come to love him. I wasn't exactly sure what he meant at the time. But as I grew older, I began to sense something in myself."

Everyone turned and looked right at David. They all had strange, surprised, smiling expressions.

"That's about it. Kevin and I got out the Ouija board several times and Ishmael basically told us the same things. After Kevin left for California, I never got out the board again."

Ken asked. "Do you still have the Ouija board?"

"Oh. No. Right after Kevin moved away, I happened to see the same gypsy people in the parking lot again. I ran home, got the board and took it to the same old gypsy lady. I asked if she'd like to buy it back again. I'd sell it at half what I paid for it since I did use it. I did show her I'd put my initials on one of the back corners. She was very nice and smiled. She told me she was sure I had learned all I was supposed to know and would gladly take the board back." Muraroot paused for a moment. "Then, she said something very strange. You should have seen the look on her face."

Ken asked. "What did she say?"

"She said she knew of someone else who needed to have the board and would come to buy it in the not too distant future. There was very important information he and a close friend needed to know. The initials on the back of the board would only reinforce the knowledge they learned was significant and would eventually help one of them put an important puzzle together." Muraroot shook his head. "I have no idea what she meant but she bought the board back from me."

Shock and surprise came to David's face and he gasped. "Oh, my God. Could it be?" He shook his head in a negative manner and waved his hand.

Everyone knew he'd explain later.

Then, the expression on Muraroot's face completely changed. He giggled. "Do you know how many Davids I met and wondered if he was the one I was supposed to remember?" He paused for a moment shaking his head. "Yeah. None of them made any major impression on me, so I knew eventually, they weren't 'the one'."

Ken continued. "All right. How about you move forward to the next time you feel there's something of importance. Do you think you can do that?"

"Ah. Okay. Yes." Muraroot's face was filled with joy. "I'm in high school. Yeah. I'm a Junior."

"Do you know what year it is?"

"Yeah. Oh. Wow! It's nineteen fifty-nine! Cool!"

"Nineteen fifty-nine? And how old are you?"

"I'm sixteen. Almost seventeen. Yeah. Totally cool. And speaking of cool, there's a hell of a lot of snow outside. Yeah. It's February."

"Tell me things you know and remember."

"I'm captain of the soccer team and we've been winning all the games we've been playing this year. Coach says I should definitely go out for soccer when I head off to college." He paused for a few seconds. "There's something I have as a secret. I can't tell anyone. I've had it for several years now."

Ken tilted his head. "Oh. What is your secret?"

Muraroot sat straight up. "Only if you promise not to tell anyone. Promise?"

"Okay. Yes. I promise."

Muraroot relaxed again and spoke in a kind of whisper. "I have realized I'm not like the others. The other guys. They're all getting crazy about the girls and talking about going out on dates. I've found I seem to be interested in… guys. Yeah. There's one guy who's almost a head shorter than me, smart, good-looking and has a terrific personality. But I haven't said anything. I think he's interested in a girl who's a Sophomore. I know I have to be careful. I don't want anyone to start calling me queer or sissy. Yeah."

Ken spoke with understanding. "That makes sense. I understand why you want it to be a secret. Not to worry. Now. There's one thing we haven't talked about yet. Where are you? Where do you live?"

"Why, in Boston! Well, just outside Boston."

Ken continued. "Very good. Thank you. Okay. Let's move forward to when you're a Senior and about to graduate. Can we move forward to your Senior Week and what is happening there?"

"Yes. There are all sorts of parties and the Senior Prom. I took Margaret to the dance. It was fun. Also, I was given an award for being one of the best soccer captains ever. I thought that was really great." He paused. "But I have to tell you about one of the parties I went to that week. Yeah. It was, man... way out! There was a lady there named Lorie. Yeah. I realized she had to be the one Ishmael had told me about back on the Ouija board. She was a psychic reader. I just had to go and talk with her. You know already I've always believed in things like Tarot Cards, Ouija boards and stuff like that." He smiled.

"Can you tell me some of the things she told you?"

Muraroot laughed. "Certainly. She started off, telling me about going to college and studying law. But then, she paused and she seemed very confused. I asked her what was wrong. She told me there was something she couldn't see. It was covered in a cloudy haze. It definitely was important but there was no way to see into the haze. After a short pause, she started again, telling me she'd try to get back to that."

"Then, she started into past lives. Wow. That was so groovy. Yeah, man. She told me there was a man who continued to show up in virtually all my significant past lives. I'd meet him in this life and his name would begin with a 'D'. He'd become very important to me. I REALLY thought that was cool. Again, I immediately realized it had to be the David, Ishmael told me to remember. It sounded like I was finally going to be able to be who I knew I was. I was glad of that."

"Then, she shook her head and told me the previous confusing cloudy issue was back. She knew something was going to happen to me. It would be of major significance. Somehow, it would lead me to get involved with some kind of native people. They'd have dark skin color and black hair. Also, a stone carving of a snake near water would be of significance."

"She sat there for a moment and shook her head. How this was going to happen was impossible for her to see. The cloudy haze was much too dense. And for some reason, she could see nothing more beyond getting involved with the native people."

"I began to wonder if I was going to die. But she smiled and looked at me very hard. She shook her head and told me not to worry as she could feel that somehow and someway things would turn out all right." He paused with a strange expression on his face.

Ken spoke. "Muraroot. Is everything okay?"

Muraroot questioned. "Who is Muraroot? Wait! My name IS Muraroot. But it isn't."

Ken instantly realized he'd never addressed Muraroot by name while talking with him in this entire session until now. "You aren't Muraroot?"

"Why, yes. But no. My real name is Mason. Mason Farley."

David's eyes grew large and his mouth fell open again. Mason Farley. 'MF'. Those WERE the initials on the back of the Ouija board.

"Mason. I'm so sorry for the confusion. Not to worry. Now, I believe we've had enough for today. We'll continue again tomorrow. How does that sound?"

"Totally cool! Groovy!" Muraroot smiled.

"Now. Tomorrow, we'll go a lot more into your life after high school. But before we end this session, I have one more question. When you come out of this session, do you want everyone to call you Muraroot or Mason? It's up to you."

Muraroot smiled and chuckled. "Now, that I know my name is really Mason, they can call me Mason. But I won't forget. I'm also Muraroot. Okay. See you later alligator!"

Ken chuckled. "Okay, Mason. I'm going to count backward

from five to one. When I reach one, you'll wake up from the session and you'll remember everything. Do you understand?"

"Yes. Cool, Daddy-O! Got it, man. I do."

Ken slowly counted from five to one and Mason came out of the session.

"Wow! My name is Mason! Wow! Totally cool! And I'm from Boston. Yeah. New England!" He turned to David. "David. Now, I understand about the snake carving and your name starts with a 'D'. And we were together in many past lives. Wow! This really is totally groovy!"

David shook his head and snickered. "Yep! Welcome to the conversation of the early nineteen sixties and Rock 'n' Roll."

Everyone broke out laughing.

Ken commented. "I have a huge feeling the cloudy haze Lorie saw was the plane crash Mason was in. And she was correct. You survived and here you are."

Ricardo turned to David. "You seemed to be quite surprised when Mason mentioned the letters he put on the back of his Ouija board. Why?"

"The Ouija board I bought, back when I was thirteen, had an 'M' and 'F' in one of the back corners. I now understand. My Ouija board was the same one Mason had."

Miguel cried out. "Wow! What are the chances? Holy Cow!"

Ricardo called out. "I do not know about you but I think that deserves lunch and definitely a cocktail. What does everyone think about that?"

David cheered. "I'm all for that! Let's go! I don't know about anyone else but I'm hungry."

They all headed down to the restaurant for a late lunch then out onto the patio for early cocktails. It was obvious Ken needed to have some explanation for many of the things he'd heard, during the session.

David called out. "I don't care if it is only two-thirty. After all I heard this morning, I need a cocktail. Hey. Somewhere in the world, it's five o'clock." He began to laugh. "Someone should write a song saying 'it's five o'clock somewhere' for occasions like this."

They all laughed as they sat down at a table on the patio.

Ken turned to Mason. "Well, Mason. How does it feel, getting to know your past?"

"So far. So good. Totally cool! But I have to admit. I'm quite apprehensive about what I still don't know. If I was from Boston, why in the hell did I get down here?"

Ken shook his head. "I know what you mean. I'm sure there has to be some explanation why you were on that plane."

David interrupted. "I'm also interested in finding out more about you. Did you have any brothers or sisters? You know. Stuff like that."

Mason smiled. "Hey! I already know that."

Ricardo was curious. "Really? But you never mentioned anything about them during your session."

"Yes. I know. But Doctor Ken wasn't asking me anything about them. I can tell you more about all that if you want to know."

David smiled. "Sure. Why not!"

"Man. Where do I begin? Humm. First off. I don't have any brothers or sisters. My dad is some bigwig of a pretty big company. It's been in the family for some time. Yeah. We're pretty well-off. I always went to a private school. One of the best in Boston. Because I did so well academically, I'm going to go to a very good private college. They have a terrific law school there and a great soccer team, too."

He paused for a moment. "I know mom and dad are concerned I haven't shown any interest in many of the eligible girls around. I never dated and taking Margaret to the Senior Prom was basically arranged. I don't know if they know." He stopped short and looked quickly at everyone with an embarrassed look on his face.

David looked right at Mason and spoke quietly. "Mason. Not to worry. It's quite all right. A lot has happened since nineteen sixty. Being gay doesn't have the same stigma it did way back then. Just sixteen years ago in June of nineteen sixty-nine, the police started raiding a gay bar in New York City and there was like a five-day standoff. It was at the Stonewall. Because of that event, the Gay Rights Movement began. The Gay Community was organized and has come a long way but there's still a long way to go. So, don't feel ashamed to express yourself. It's a whole new world. Even the black folks got recognized in nineteen sixty-three with the Civil Rights Movement and Martin Luther King, Junior. Seriously. Trust me. One of these days, they might even legalize same-sex marriage. But don't hold your breath on that one."

Everyone gave sounds of agreement.

Mason was surprised. "Seriously? So, it's all right to talk about being gay? Gay? It's called being gay?"

Ricardo grinned and raised his hand.

Mason looked over at Ricardo. "Ricardo! You?"

Then, Ken raised his hand. "I have many patients in Atlanta who are so glad I'm gay. It makes them feel more at ease. And you'd be surprised at how many straight people don't mind coming to a gay psychiatrist. Many of them have told me I seem to be more sensitive, attentive and in tune."

Then, Miguel looked at everyone with a Cheshire grin on his face. "No, guys. I am a straight guy. I like women but I am single because I just like being single. I like to be able to do what I want, when I want to do it and not be hampered with strings attached. I like what I do and it keeps me busy and I like my life. Yeah."

Mason started to laugh. "You mean to tell me that four out of five of us here are..." He bent his head down and spoke very quietly. "Gay?"

They all erupted in loud raucous laughter.

Miguel smiled. "I must be honest. I love working with gay guys. They are always creative, helpful and upfront. They also have incredible ideas and thinking. I have found that gay guys can be the best of friends. And you guys. Wow. I consider myself lucky to know all of you here and know that I consider you all as good friends and I hope it continues that way."

Ken raised his glass in the air. "To good friends. Hear! Hear!"

All raised their glasses, clinking them together while laughing and crying out. "Hear! Hear!" "Hear! Hear!"

That night before going to bed, Mason turned to David. "David. I can't tell you how much I appreciate what you're doing for me. I must admit, it's a bit scary. I sure hope I don't turn out to be some axe murderer. And I was coming down here to escape being put in jail."

David laughed. "I seriously doubt that. But I do understand. I believe Ken is doing a great job at helping you. And now that we know your name, we can start checking to see about your family in Boston."

Michael called out. "Well, I'm sure glad his name is Mason Farley and not Mother Fucker like YOU thought it might be." He looked right at James with a Cheshire grin on his face.

The entire room exploded in laughter.

James shook his head. "Only Michael would remember that. Only Michael."

Everyone continued to laugh.

Michael continued. "Damn. For it to be the SAME Ouija board. That's fantastic and creepy at the same time. Geez. And that Ishmael. He really got around. I just might have to get a Ouija board and see what he might be able to tell me. HEY! He might give me some great lottery numbers or maybe even the name of my next ex-husband!"

This brought the whole room to loud raucous laughter again. It took a few minutes for it to finally calm down.

Then, Michael cried out again. "Wait! You said Ricardo is visiting with David and Mason? David wants Ricardo to meet me. Well. Maybe HE is supposed to be my next ex-husband?"

Everyone just broke into more loud laughter one more time.

Soon, James continued. "I must tell you. I had invited Doctor Ken Johnson to the party tonight but he was not going to be in town. He told me to express how sorry he was that he wasn't going to be here."

He paused for a moment then continued. "Yes. The door to Mason's past was slowly beginning to open. David finally understood what Lorie had told him about the two letters of 'M' and 'F'." He quickly looked directly at Michael with an evil eye.

This brought the room to a burst of roaring laughter once again.

CHAPTER XIII

James turned to everyone in the room. "Is everyone still comfortable? There's still plenty of food and cocktails. If anyone needs to run to the 'little room', please feel free to do so. We can take a short break as I get something to eat, too."

After about fifteen minutes, James stood by the fireplace and continued his story. "Yes. David called me the very next day and asked me if I'd do some research into a family named Farley located in the Boston area. I told him I'd check into it immediately."

"James. How's the connection? Can you hear me all right?"

"Hear you fine. What's up?"

"I'm sorry I haven't gotten to you sooner but things have been rather hectic here. We're in Rio de Janeiro and trying to get information here. Staying at a great hotel on the beach. You're not going to believe what's happened. I was hoping you'd do some research for me and see if you can find a family in Boston called Farley."

"Farley. In Boston? I'll see what I can do. So, what else has been going on? Ah. Wait a minute. You said 'we'. What's this 'WE'?"

David paused for a moment. "I met this guy down here..."

"WHAT!? You have to go all the way to Brazil to meet a guy?" James started laughing loudly.

"Would you please wait a minute? Let me explain. Geez. Now,

think back. You remember back, during our Senior Week in high school and we went to that party? Where we met that woman called Lorie? Well. All that stuff has come true. He was living here with a native tribe out in the boonies."

James was surprised. "Oh, my God! The one with the letters 'M' and 'F'? Is it possible it's the same guy I've seen a few news clips about on TV? Really? I think they said his name was something like some 'root'."

David was shocked. "You've got to be kidding? The story's already in the states!? Holy cow! Yes. He's the one. We're trying to find out information about him. I'm sure the information in the report is totally incomplete."

"Well, they did say he has amnesia and has no idea of his history prior to a plane crash there. Must tell you from the pictures they've shown on the news reports, ugly doesn't know his name or where he lives."

"Wow. Wait till you hear his whole story. I called my doctor in Atlanta and asked him to refer me to a psychiatrist there. He recommended Doctor Kenneth Johnson."

James responded. "Yes. I met him at a cocktail party one time. Seemed like a really nice guy. Did you get in contact with him? Why did you need a psychiatrist?"

"I did. And he actually has come down here to help out and is staying in the same hotel. He's been putting Mason under hypnosis since he couldn't remember anything prior to getting here. So far, so good. There's still more to be found out. Will let you know. That's how I know his real name. Mason Farley. Yeah. Remember those initials on the back of the Ouija board I used to have? Those were HIS initials. 'MF'. Yeah. My Ouija board was once his."

"No shit! You can't be serious? No way?"

"Yep. I was totally blown away when it came out in his session. Yeah."

"Wow. Okay. Will check into this for you. I'll let you know as soon as I find out something. How's your money holding out? You need me to wire you any?"

"James. Thanks. But I'm fine so far. I appreciate your help. You're a great friend as usual. Take care and we'll see you as soon as much of this is straightened out. Got to run. It's just about time for another of Mason's hypnosis sessions. Take care. Later. Later."

David was correct. It was time to go to Ken's room for another session. Everyone headed that way.

Soon, all resumed their places in the room. Shortly, Mason was under.

Ken began. "Mason. We're going to continue where we left off in our last session. Is that clear?"

"Yes. Not a problem. Cool." He paused for a moment. "After graduation, summer was rather hectic, getting ready to go off to college. Have to tell you. Just before leaving, I've been invited to a really groovy party."

"Tell me about the party."

"A lot of my friends are here. I know it's going to be a blast. Yeah. Oh! Wow! Oh. Yeah. There's my dance. I love it." Mason starts wiggling in the bed and singing. "Yeah, baby. Let's do the Twist." He starts to laugh.

David, Miguel and Ricardo began to chuckle.

Ken turns to them with a questioning look on his face.

Ricardo whispers. "We'll explain later."

Ken returns to Mason. "So, you like the Twist?"

Mason stops gyrating in the bed. "Oh. Yeah. It's the hit dance of nineteen sixty right now." He has a big smile on his face. "Everyone's doing it." He pauses. "Oh. Someone's making a toast. Yeah."

Ken questions. "Mason. What's the toast for?"

"It's for Jack Kennedy. I'm sure everyone here is going to vote for him. We're all old enough and it'll be the first time we get to vote. We really like him and it's not just because he's from Massachusetts."

Ken continues. "Okay. Now, if you don't mind, let's move on. To college."

"Went to Freshman orientation and met a lot of new people. Also, signed up for the soccer team. Seems the coach was familiar with my abilities, during high school and was really glad to have me on the team. The teachers are terrific and my classes are going well. Everyone's ecstatic Jack Kennedy won and will be the next president." He paused. "Mom and dad threw a terrific Christmas party. Everyone was interested in how my classes were going."

"Something really cool has happened. My team members have elected me captain. Imagine that. Eighteen and captain of my college soccer team. They all said I was such a good player and I also happen to be the biggest guy on the team." Mason paused for a moment. "Have to tell you. Coach and the president of the school got with all family members of the guys on the team and said they've arranged for us to do something really groovy this coming summer."

"Mason? What is it?"

"We're going to play soccer! Yeah! They contacted several universities in Central and South American countries and lined up several soccer games with about ten universities. That should be a total blast. Yeah. Friendly hands across borders."

Ken turned to look at David, Miguel and Ricardo. He could see it on their faces. It was now obvious to all why Mason was in South America.

Mason continued. "When Freshman year ended in early June, everyone on the team was getting ready for a summer of soccer. Our first game would be in Mexico City at the end of June, a week later in Bogotá and from there, we're going to Rio de Janeiro. I can't remember where we're going from that point. I think Buenos Aires. Coach, several school officials, some chaperons and an interpreter who speaks Spanish and Portuguese are going to be along."

Ken spoke softly. "Mason. From this point on, it might be extremely difficult to talk about. We now understand why you were in Brazil. If you'd prefer not to recount what happened, you don't have to."

Mason began to shake. "I sense there's something terrible about to happen. I can just feel it. It's like there's a thick haze I'm trying to see through. I must go and find out what's in and beyond the haze. I need to face my demon. I now believe it's the cloudy haze Lorie couldn't see into."

David looked over at Ken and whispered. "Ken. Could this be dangerous for Mason? I don't want him to go into any mental trauma."

Ken whispered. "I believe he's more than strong enough to face what he's about to see and experience and tell us. I know if he doesn't, he'll always wonder what happened."

David's face was filled with fear. "Ken. I love this man. If anything should happen to him, my heart will break."

Ricardo reached over and patted David on the back. He whispered. "I believe Doctor Ken is correct. Mason needs to face his demon. He needs to know. He is going to be all right."

Ken spoke softly. "Mason. What did Lorie say about the haze?"

"She said she couldn't see into it but she knew I was going to be all right on the other side. I know I must find out and do it."

"Very good. We're now going to go to the place where you're leaving Bogotá and heading to Rio de Janeiro. Do you understand?"

Mason smiled. "Yes, Doctor Ken. Yes, I do."

"Then, you may continue."

Mason started to laugh. "You should see us all, trying to get on the bus. The hotel has arranged to have a bus take all of us to the airport early enough, so we'd have plenty of time. The plane leaves at eight."

"Finally, we arrived at the airport, got through all that immigration stuff and got seated at the gate. Yeah. Bob and I are sitting together. He asked if I wanted something. Yeah. We had to leave so early and no one got to eat any breakfast. I heard they're going to give us something on the plane. Hey! It's a nine-hour flight."

"Hey! Farley! Want something to drink? I'm going to run and get a soda." Bob got up from his seat.

"No. I'm fine. But thanks for asking." I looked at Bob and smiled. Bob is a cool guy. He and I have become really good friends. Met him when I joined the soccer team at school last fall.

After a while, Bob returned with his cola and sat in a seat across from me. He quickly looked around at the other people, sitting at the gate, waiting to board the plane. "Well, Farley. What have you thought of the trip so far? I think it's been totally cool."

I told him I was really pleased we got to do this. Trips like this didn't happen every day. And what an adventure.

"Yeah. I'm sure glad we have an interpreter with us. I understand coach speaks some. I'd sure hate for us to come across as the ugly Americans." Bob gave a big grin.

I thought it was great we were getting to play with teams who really knew the game and also getting to meet guys our own age from foreign countries.

Bob took a drink of his cola. "I think it's so groovy. Let's see. Our next game is the day after tomorrow. That'll give us a chance to rest up for a day after we get there later this evening." He paused for a moment. "Plane was supposed to leave at eight this morning. How much more time is it before we board?"

I was pretty sure it would be leaving in less than thirty minutes. I noticed there were several people, looking at the clock on the wall. Guess they were wondering how close we were to boarding. With it being a nine-hour flight and a two-hour difference in time between here and there, we'd be getting in around seven that evening in Rio.

Bob turned around and looked at several of those in the group. "I'm surprised there aren't more people. Looks like only eight other people so far besides all of us. We'll virtually have the whole plane to ourselves. I think that's so cool."

Personally, I was looking forward to catching some shut-eye during the flight. Finally, there was an announcement. Everyone grabbed their carry-on luggage and headed out the door.

Shortly, we were at the plane and climbing the steps to the door. It didn't take long for all of us to get seated.

Bob noticed where I was sitting. "Farley! On all the flights we've taken, you seem to choose a seat in the same area of the plane every time. What is that?"

He was referring to the seats near the wings. I told him I'd heard it was the strongest part of the airplane. Not that I was expecting anything bad to happen. It just gave me a little reassurance. I took a window seat and buckled myself in.

When the engines started up and the plane began to slowly move forward, Bob looked out the window. He was sitting right behind me. "Wonder how many RPMs those propellers turn?"

I began to laugh and said. "I don't know. Just as long as it's fast enough to keep us in the air."

Our comments had everyone on the plane laughing.

The plane had been aloft for just over two hours when Bob turned to his right and looked out the window. "Farley. Check out your window. Looks like one wingding dilly of a storm, coming up from the south. And look at all the lightning."

Just then, an announcement came over the intercom system. It was from the pilot. I was sure he was speaking Spanish but possibly Portuguese.

Our interpreter understood, got up and stood in the aisle. "The captain was just explaining. They're going to divert to the north to try and avoid the upcoming storm. He also said he was sorry that it will delay our arrival somewhat. He wants everyone to fasten your seat belt." He returned to his seat.

Even though the plane changed course, the storm quickly caught up with it. I couldn't believe how incredibly fierce it was. The plane was being tossed around like a rag doll. Up and down and sideways. With every major jerk, everyone let out a cry of anxiety. It was extremely disconcerting.

Suddenly, the plane jerked violently and Rick, who was sitting back and across the aisle from me, was thrown out of his seat and landed in the aisle. He hadn't put on his seat belt correctly and it had come loose. Rick let out a loud groan.

Bob yelled out. "Farley! I think Rick's hurt!"

I got up, grabbed Rick off the floor and put him back in his seat again. Made sure he was buckled in tight. I told Bob I thought he'd be okay and started to return to my seat. Just then, the plane tossed violently, throwing me up against the ceiling then back down onto the floor. My head hit pretty hard, causing me to yell really loud.

"Farley!" Bob cried out. He and another teammate quickly got up, pulled me off the floor and strapped me tightly in the seat on the aisle. It was easier than putting me back in my original window seat. They quickly got back to their own seats and strapped in.

I made a joke about what happened even though the knot on my head hurt like hell.

Bob responded. "Glad you're okay. You got a nice bump on the head."

The plane continued to lurch and jerk, being severely tossed around for at least an hour. It was so bad, no one said much of anything.

Suddenly, I began to hear the loud sounds of twisting metal and rivets popping. The sound was terrifying. I knew this was NOT a good thing. Shortly, I realized, I was absolutely correct. Right before my very eyes, the plane began to disintegrate and come apart.

I heard Bob scream out. "FARLEY!"

Mason spoke in a nervous voice. "At that, the plane came completely to pieces, tossing everyone out into the sky and into the darkness of the horrendous storm. I was still strapped in the seat and was being tossed around in the wind as I started falling to earth. It seemed like forever as the wind blew me up and down in the air. I'm not sure but I think something hit me in the head because I don't remember anything after that." Mason paused. "The next thing I remember is waking up and there was a native man, looking down at me. And he called me Muraroot."

Ken spoke quietly. "Mason. I want you to relax right now and calm yourself. Everything is fine. You've come through the storm. Literally. You now understand who you are and why you're here. Just relax." He turned to the others. "Now, we know. I believe all questions have now been answered."

He then turned back to Mason. "Mason. I know you have just come through a very traumatic experience. I do want you to remember it but I also want you to remember it happened a very long time ago. When I bring you out of this session, I want you to talk with me or David or any of the others about any or all of the information you've learned in all of these sessions. Since you wanted all of them to be here, they all understand your past and what you've been through. Just as before, I'll count backward slowly from five to one and when I reach one, you'll come out. Do you understand?"

"Yes, Doctor Ken. I do."

Shortly, Mason was out of the session and sat there, shaking his head. Tears began to stream down his face. "They are dead. All my friends. Everyone is dead." He began to cry.

David jumped up and ran over to the bed, hugging Mason. "It's all right. It's all right. You're all right."

Mason finally calmed down. "Wow. What a bummer. That was scary as all get out. Damn. And… I lost all my teammates. Coach. Everyone else. Wow." Sorrow filled his face.

Ricardo shook his head. "That was incredible. How traumatic. It really is amazing you survived."

David agreed. "Damn! I don't know about any of you but I sure as hell could use a drink. Any takers?"

Everyone present raised their hand.

Mason turned to Ken. "You think I'll need to go under anymore?"

"Mason. I believe we've hit the major high points of things necessary for you to remember. I'll be here for just a few more days to make sure. If you still feel there are some blank spaces, we can address those later on."

Little did David know but James had immediately contacted a reporter friend who worked at a local TV station, telling him his best friend was the one who discovered the man living with the natives in Brazil. He told James to tell him all he knew. After hearing the story, he immediately arranged a trip to interview David and Mason.

CHAPTER XIV

James took a sip of his cocktail. "I had no idea Donald was going to rush down there to get a jump on the story." He looked over at one of the guys in the room. "I know many of you know Donald and his partner, Fred."

Donald and Fred smiled and tipped their heads in acknowledgment. Donald responded. "Hey. You know I'm always going to go after a good story. Definitely try to get there before the 'Big Guys' if you know what I mean."

Positive sounds came from the room.

James continued. "Yep. Donald was right on it. Arrived in Rio two days later. What can I say?"

Everyone was sitting out on the patio of the hotel when one of the clerks from the front desk came out and walked up to the table. "Señor David. There are several men at the front desk, wanting to talk with you. The one named Donald told me to tell you he is a friend of James. He said you would understand."

David smiled, got up from his chair and turned to the rest. "Okay. No. I don't understand. I give up. No clue who they are. But if he knows James, this should be very interesting. I'll be back, shortly." He followed the desk clerk to the lobby.

Donald saw David approaching and extended his hand. "Hello, David. I'm Donald. I'm a friend of James. This is Fred, my partner.

Ralph, here, is my cameraman. I'm a TV reporter. James told me your story. Well, the part he knew, about the man you found here. I hope it isn't presumptuous of me to have come but I'd truly like to interview you and Mason and the others involved with the story. James made it sound so incredible. I must admit. I'd seen a very short snippet, regarding Mason that came across on one of the national news affiliates. They only had a brief report that raised a million questions. And they were calling him Muraroot."

David smiled. "Donald, Fred, Ralph, welcome. Have you had lunch? Where are you staying?"

Donald shook his head. "To answer your questions. No. We haven't had lunch and two, we just arrived and haven't found a place to stay yet."

David was totally taken aback. "Wow! You REALLY ARE a reporter. No food. No lodging. It's the story. The story comes first!"

They all laughed.

David grabbed Donald's arm. "Come. You all will stay here. It'll make it easier to talk and enjoy each other's company." He led them to the front desk.

After they all got signed in, Ralph went out to the front doorman and directed him to the rooms they'd be staying in. The doorman would bring their luggage up immediately. He rejoined the rest who were waiting for him.

David left a large tip at the front desk. "Please, give this to Jose when he's done taking their things up to their rooms. Thank you."

Donald turned to David and smiled. "David. Thank you but I could've done that. I have an expense account."

David smiled. "Well. Okay. But I'll cover anything your station won't. How does that sound?"

Fred made a fist and thrust his right arm into the air. "Perfect!"

Everyone roared with laughter as they headed out onto the patio.

Walking up to the table, David made introductions all around. Two of the waiters immediately pulled up another table and chairs, so all would be able to sit as a group. David also asked them to take orders for the three new members of the group. Then, they all sat down.

David turned to Donald. "So. James told you about us down here. And Mason's real name. How did you know where we were?"

Donald nodded. "James said you had Doctor Kenneth Johnson here, so I called his office and found out the name of the hotel here in Rio. Easy as pie."

Donald looked over at Mason. "I have to tell you. Your story is part of some of the major news in the states right now. What's so interesting is it just raised so many questions. They don't even know your real name. It's now obvious to me the 'Big Guys' have no idea how or where to contact you or they'd have been sitting here instead of me. If not for David's friend, James, I wouldn't be here, either. Something tells me this is going to be a huge story. Huge. And I'd love to be the one to bring it back to the states."

Mason smiled. "Well, you really have to thank these guys for making it happen. If not for them, I'd still be out there, holding a spear, thinking my name was Muraroot with no clue about my history."

Drinks arrived and food shortly thereafter. While they ate, Donald wanted to hear something about each of everyone sitting there. Ricardo and Miguel told some of their stories. When Ken started, Donald held up his hand. "I already know all about you, Doctor Johnson. You're one of the most renowned and prestigious psychiatrists in Atlanta. But I do want to know why you're here? We'll get to that when I do some extensive interviews with all of you. That's why I wanted to hear something now, so I'll know what to ask while we're filming."

"When would you like to start your interviews?" David paused. "I'm sorry. Stupid me. You're a reporter. The STORY comes first!"

This made everyone burst out laughing.

Donald shook his head. "I see, David totally understands. If you all don't mind, I'd like to start in just a little while. Ralph can get his equipment set up and once that's done, we can start. I do have a feeling it'll probably go into tomorrow. I hope that's all right with everyone."

Sounds of approval came from all sitting at the table.

Donald bent his head down and after a moment raised it again. "This sounds a bit presumptuous but I just have a really good feeling about this, especially for me. After I submit my first short report to the station and tell them what this whole thing really means, they just might let me do a special report. Yeah. That would be one big feather in my hat."

Mason added. "Yes. You just might want to go see where it all started in Barcelos. Maybe even go see the ancient ruins in the cliffs and meet my father and his tribe. Possibly even go see the wreckage of the plane."

Donald's mouth fell open. "Oh, my God! Mason! You know, you're right! There's a HUGE story here!" He paused. "And not only here." He paused again with a huge smile on his face. "But in Boston as well. Wouldn't it be amazing to find your parents if they're still alive and film your reunion with them? WOW! This IS amazing! Once I do my interviews with all of you, I'll have an idea as to the road I need to take to make this whole story happen and in a logical order. Yep! ONE HOUR SPECIAL!" He broke out laughing. He stopped short and turned to everyone. "Please, say it's all right with you all?"

Everyone had huge grins on their faces and started clapping and cheering.

Donald jumped up and cried out. "YES!!!"

David clapped his hands. "Just think of the publicity it'll bring to you, Ricardo, as a major tour guide in Brazil. And you, Miguel. Everyone will be wanting to charter your helicopter. Doctor Ken, folks will come to you just so they can hear your story." He began to snicker. "And I'll bet you just might be able to write a book about all this."

Everyone cheered and clapped their hands again.

David continued. "Mason, you're going to be doing lecture

tours, telling everyone your story and about living with your tribe all those years. And teaching their language. Yep. I think everyone is going to benefit from all this."

Mason turned to David. "And what about you? You deserve something."

David smiled and looked lovingly at Mason. "I've been the luckiest of all. I have found an incredible man who I love dearly and I have enough ideas for paintings to last me several lifetimes." David stood up and raised his glass. "To the success of us all."

They all stood, raising their glasses, clinking them together. "Hear! Hear!" They cheered. "Hear! Hear!"

Mason put his glass back on the table and looked at David. "Put your glass down."

David placed his glass on the table just as Mason walked over and hugged David tightly. "I love you so much, you silly goose."

Little did they realize but everyone sitting on the patio had been listening to what was being said. It had become clear they were seeing the actual people they had seen in the news reports by the local TV reporter, Marco. Everyone there stood up, applauding, whistling and cheering.

James acknowledged one of the guests. "Donald. If you'd like to elaborate on what took place because of your visit? You can come up here or stay comfortable where you are."

Donald smiled. "James. If you don't mind, I really would like to remain seated here in this comfortable chair." He looked around the room. "I'm sure everyone can hear me just as well as me standing up there."

The shaking of the heads in the room affirmed Donald's comment.

"Well. I must tell you. After the interviews, Ralph made a master tape and we sent it by special messenger to the station here in Atlanta. I wasn't going to leave until I heard from the manager. If he did a 'thumbs-down', I was going to be on the next plane out. A 'thumbs-up' meant I was given the 'OK' to continue."

He looked over at James. "You called me and told me you saw the report accompanied by my manager's comments afterward, indicating there was more to come. This was confirmed by a call from my manager the next day. Yep. That was the signal I needed. James, you found Mason's parents in no time and explained to them the national report that aired was about their son."

James nodded. "Yes. I told them he most likely wouldn't be able to leave Brazil for some time due to no passport or proper paperwork. I wasn't surprised they booked the first flight down to Rio to see their Mason."

Donald smiled. "Ralph, Fred and I, along with everyone else, were there to greet them when they arrived. Any one of you who saw my special knows how wonderful it was."

Michael raised his hand. "I remember it. It was amazing how Mason's parents actually got to meet his native father and the tribe. It was very emotional how his mom expressed how much she appreciated the chief taking care of Mason and calling him his son. That was so special. I guess the tribe has been resettled by now. Your special report showed the construction going on."

Donald continued. "Yes, they've moved into their new complex and they're slowly getting to assimilate into the ways and culture of those in Barcelos. They really like the access to education and healthcare."

James jumped in. "As many of you know, David and Mason now live at the house on the beach in Mexico but they make trips down to Barcelos once in a while to check on things. I do remember all Mason had to go through to get his US passport and all the paperwork it took. I swear. I think it's because he was so famous, Brazil gave him an honorary citizenship."

Everyone clapped their hands in approval.

Donald continued. "Yes. Over the last couple of years, David and Mason have accomplished a lot in the area down there. They're constantly traveling back and forth from their home in Mexico to Barcelos to make sure everything is going smoothly for the tribe. They have also visited Mason's parents in Boston several times. Mason has become quite the celebrity."

He shook his head and grinned. "Several modeling firms in New York contacted Mason, wanting him to do some modeling for them. They'd been looking for someone around his age who wasn't only sexy and handsome but mature and oozing with masculinity. Yeah. Him being the famous man from the Brazilian jungle, they were willing to pay big bucks."

"He got an agent who sets a schedule for him that's to his liking. He not only does modeling for designer clothes but he also does ads as you well know. I'm sure most of you if not all of you have seen the beer commercial he does."

Everyone in the room shook their heads and smiled, making sounds of approval. "Yeah." "You bet."

James raised his hand. "Donald. Hope you don't mind me interrupting but I did want to mention this. Mason knew he was from a well-to-do family but he had no idea how well-to-do it was. His parents had established a very large trust for him and never dismantled it, not knowing the true fate of their son. It was obvious Mason really never had to go to work but he enjoyed doing the commercial ads and modeling. It was fun for him. And of course, not being a stupid man, he let ME invest much of his money from work, making him even more."

Michael cried out. "Seriously, People! If you haven't let James do some investing for you, you're an absolute imbecile. He's made me a very well-off man. Very well-off. The gods have smiled on James, giving him the ability to invest extremely wisely." He smiled and raised his glass in the air.

Everyone in the room raised their glasses in the air and cried out. "Hear! Hear!"

James smiled at Michael. "Michael. Thank you very much. I'll pay you later for that wonderful verbal advertisement."

Everyone just howled as Michael stood and took a few bows.

He looked over at Donald. "Sorry for interrupting. Please, continue."

Donald smiled. "Not a problem." He paused for a moment. "One thing David and Mason had done was place a granite memorial marker and bronze plaque at the site of the crash. It was airlifted in, using Miguel's helicopter and placed near the tail section of the plane. It contained information about the soccer team, where it was from and all the names of those with the soccer team who died. It also contained the names of the other passengers and crew. Once installed, photographs were taken and sent to all family members of those who died in the crash."

James raised his hand again. "Sorry for interrupting again but I'll tell you. Miguel and Ricardo have both been sending me money to invest for them. Happy to say they're both building quite nice little nest eggs. I'll also tell you this. And I hope I'm not breaking a confidence. Miguel and Ricardo don't know it. David and Mason, both, have been contributing money to be invested for them. David and Mason told me if they should ever ask where the extra money came from, I was to tell them it was from anonymous donors who had seen the TV Specials and reports. Just to let you know how considerate and kind both of them are."

Donald continued. "I just might check with upper management and hear their thoughts on a possible update special. I think it might even help the charity fund that's been set up to help the tribe. Since David and Mason will be here shortly, I'll be able to speak directly to them about recent events."

—∞—

At that moment, a car pulled up and parked down the street from the home of James and Albert. David, Mason and Ricardo got out of the car and finally began to walk up the sidewalk to the house. David stopped and grabbed Mason's arm. He looked up into his face and smiled. "If you only knew how much I love you."

Mason smiled and looked down into David's face. "If you only knew how much I love you, you silly goose. If not for you, I'd have lived my life alone. You've brought me into a world and shown me more than I could have ever imagined. Because of you, I found myself. I know who I really am. It would never have happened if not for you." He pulled David to him and hugged him tightly.

Ricardo called out. "Okay, guys. Break it up. Let us get a move on. We are late already." He began to snicker.

David and Mason both began to chuckle as well.

They all walked up to the house and David rang the bell.

Albert heard the bell and turned to everyone. "I believe the guests of honor have finally arrived."

Everyone applauded and cheered.

Albert opened the door. "Gentlemen! Welcome! Nice to see you again. And Ricardo. A warm welcome to you. So glad you could come."

They walked in and were greeted by the many guests. Shortly thereafter, they reached Michael.

David looked at Michael and smiled. "Ricardo. THIS is Michael." He paused. "Remember? The one I told you about?"

Ricardo gave a big smile. "Michael, nice to meet you."

Michael smiled as he looked up into Ricardo's face. "Well. HELLO, RICARDO! And where have YOU been hiding all my life?" He immediately turned to everyone in the room and loudly shouted out. "I know he speaks English, but does anyone know how to say 'Hello. I think I'm in love' in Portuguese? I don't want there to be any mistake. Oh, Yeah!"

The room was filled with roaring laughter.

—m—

One late September day sixteen years earlier, an old gypsy lady walked into a Midtown thrift shop, checking things out. She went over to a glass-top cabinet and looked down into it. There, she saw something that piqued her interest. A big smile filled her face. She spoke in a whisper. "Ah. There you are. I've been looking for you for quite some time now."

The attendant saw her and came over. "Yes, ma'am. May I help you?"

She nodded. "Yes. I'd like to purchase this, please." She looked down into the cabinet and pointed with her right hand.

The attendant looked down. "Oh. The Ouija board?" He smiled.

She smiled back. "Yes, young man. The Ouija board."

The End

135

Printed in the United States
by Baker & Taylor Publisher Services